From the rear of the ruins, the Apaches had succeeded in their suicide charge. Tomahawks and war clubs cracked open the skulls of a few gunmen, spraying blood and muck and brain matter through the air . . . Ki, Captain Frederick and the sheriff directed barking bursts of weapons fire . . .

An Apache let fly an arrow. There was a shrill scream from across the room. Ki saw the sheriff tumble, the arrow speared through his eye. On foot, Apaches began leaping over the rubble, breaking the defensive perimeter in greater numbers . . .

DON'T MISS THESE
ALL-ACTION WESTERN SERIES
FROM THE BERKLEY PUBLISHING GROUP

THE GUNSMITH by J. R. Roberts
Clint Adams was a legend among lawmen, outlaws, and ladies. They called him . . . the Gunsmith.

LONGARM by Tabor Evans
The popular long-running series about U.S. Deputy Marshal Long—his life, his loves, his fight for justice.

LONE STAR by Wesley Ellis
The blazing adventures of Jessica Starbuck and the martial arts master, Ki. Over eight million copies in print.

SLOCUM by Jake Logan
Today's longest-running action western. John Slocum rides a deadly trail of hot blood and cold steel.

→← WESLEY ELLIS →←

LONE STAR

ON THE HANGMAN'S TRAIL

J
JOVE BOOKS, NEW YORK

LONE STAR ON THE HANGMAN'S TRAIL

A Jove Book / published by arrangement with
the author

PRINTING HISTORY
Jove edition / July 1993

ISBN: 0-515-11137-6

Jove Books are published by The Berkley Publishing Group,
200 Madison Avenue, New York, New York 10016.
The name "JOVE" and the "J" logo
are trademarks belonging to Jove Publications, Inc.

PRINTED IN THE UNITED STATES OF AMERICA

10 9 8 7 6 5 4 3 2 1

ON THE
HANGMAN'S TRAIL

Chapter 1

The long, curved blade of the *katana* winked sunlight before razor-sharp steel sliced through rope and cut the hanging man from the oak tree. The corpse thudded to the hard-packed earth and rolled down the embankment, to splash in the creek that wound through the rugged hills of southwest Texas known as the Trans-Pecos region. Jessica Starbuck and her longtime bodyguard and companion, Ki, sat astride their black geldings in grim silence.

The burning cobalt sky of midafternoon was awash in a black sea of freewheeling buzzards. Oak trees flanking the banks of the creek rustled with maybe two dozen more large scavenger birds. Some spread their wings and took to the sky at the intrusion of human life, while others, in seeming greed and arrogance, feasted with ravenous beaks and talons on the bodies of six other men in spurs and chaps who had been hung by the neck. Less than a dozen yards from Jessie, two coyotes savaged the body of still another dead man. It was about all she could stomach. Angered

1

at the sight of the desecration, Jessie unleathered her .38-caliber Colt from its holster, tied down to her thigh, and pumped one round into each coyote's head, killing them where they ate, draping their carcasses over the ravaged dead.

As Jessie holstered her iron, the geldings nickered at the loud echo of the killing shots. And black clouds of flies, swarming over the dead, buzzed up and down the creek.

Another tight moment's scrutiny of the carnage, then Jessie and Ki gently urged their mounts ahead, the geldings' hooves splashing down into the creek. One by one, with swift strokes of the *katana*, the half-American half-Japanese warrior cut each hanging cowboy free, their bodies tumbling down the bank. They didn't have time to bury the dead, Jessie knew, but they could at least give the dead some dignity. Finally, Ki slid the sword of the samurai into the scabbard thrust inside his sash. He looked at Jessie, somber.

"Something tells me we're going to be too late to save your friend and his family."

A bitter sorrow filled Jessie. She was afraid Ki was right, but until she saw it with her own eyes, she would cling to the hope that they were alive and unharmed. Nodding to herself, she surveyed the deathbed some more as buzzards flapped and squawked for the sky. The mere sight of this gruesome carnage sent a chill down her spine. The men who had done this were tough, mean, and as cunning and vicious as any outlaws they had ever come across. Jessie had to stroke the neck of her mount for a moment to keep the gelding from becoming completely spooked by the sight and smell of death and bolting the creek in a panic.

"I only wish I'd gotten his wire sooner than yesterday," she told Ki. "Bruce Southerland's a good man; he was a good friend of my father's. He has a wife and three sons; they've always been like a second family to me. May God help the bastards who did this when we catch up to them."

Through a narrowed gaze, Ki looked at a corpse floating beside his mount. "I don't understand how these men could have gone to their deaths so easily. They were tough cattlehands, surely experienced with a gun. Unless . . ."

And Jessie saw the same thing Ki saw. There were bullet holes in the backs of two corpses near them; then she spotted the bullet-shattered skull of a body floating past her.

"They were shot first, probably bushwhacked," Jessie said, "then strung up. A message. I don't know who these men were, but we passed a ranch an hour ago, and there wasn't a soul there. These men were probably the ranch hands from there. But there were signs of a struggle and a gunfight back at that ranch. They must've killed them, then brought them here. I don't know why. Who can tell what goes through the twisted minds of cold-blooded killers?"

Ki nodded several times, his lips a thin slash of tightly controlled rage. "Yeah. The Grimm brothers, Judd and Eli, with a little help from a convict friend named Bob 'Snake' Feller."

"Three real gentle souls. Their first day out of prison was today, according to Bruce Southerland's message—it looks like they mean to wipe out every one they hold responsible for sending them away. Only the Grimm brothers were guilty of robbery. They did their time, five years' worth, but now . . . now they'll be doing time in hell if they've harmed Bruce Southerland and his family."

Ki looked out across the gently rolling plain, toward the jagged hills east. "The town of Goodwill is what, maybe a half day's ride from here? That was where the trial was held, right?"

"They won't go there; they're crazy and mean, but they can't take on a whole town. No, Mr. Southerland was the jury foreman; they'll head straight for his ranch from here. Come on, Ki, there's no time to waste."

They guided their mounts out onto the baking plain. Jessie's brown Stetson and Ki's black Stetson shielded their faces from the life-sucking wrath of the sun. Jessie wore a white silk blouse and broken-in denim Levi's, the outfit hugging the shapely curves of a voluptuous body that could make men anywhere burn in lust and women gnash their teeth in envy. Behind the square belt buckle with the Circle S insignia, she hid a .38-caliber derringer with ivory grips. Aside from his samurai sword, Ki had a .44 Remington in a tied-down holster and a .44 Winchester rifle in a saddle scabbard. He was dressed in Levi's, a collarless cotton shirt, and a brown leather vest loaded with *shurikens*, throwing stars.

They had come prepared.

To manhunt.

Or outfitted to kill.

Fate would make the call.

Through a slit-eyed gaze, his almond eyes burning with bitter anger, Ki looked at Jessie as they rode hard across the plain.

Jessie felt Ki's concerned stare boring into her. She had told him all about Bruce Southerland, how the Southerland family used to spend holidays with her and her father when she was a little girl. She was fond of the Southerland family, and Ki knew this. She was afraid of what she might find at the family's spread.

She hoped for the best.

Several hard-ridden miles later they discovered the worst.

Pillars of black smoke towered into the sky, smudging the azure horizon with a dire warning of still more death, just beyond the rise. Quickly, Jessie and Ki climbed the rise and reined their mounts in at the edge of the hill.

And they stared down at the Southerland ranch.

Or, rather, what was left of it.

Fire had been set to the big oak house and the livery stables, and a swirling firestorm breathed mountainous walls of flames high above the spread. Far to the south, cattle and horses were moving pell-mell away from the inferno. The hot, smoke-choked air was rife with the stench of roasting flesh. Rage and grief filled Jessie as she watched the house where she'd eaten many a meal with the Southerland family groan under the feeding wrath of fire. There wasn't any sign of human life.

Then Jessie spotted the figure, crawling across the ground, to the east, away from the fire.

"Come on, Ki," she said, urging her mount down the rise. From a dozen yards away, she recognized Bruce Southerland. His white shirt was drenched in blood, tattered with bullet holes, his once iron-gray hair soaked crimson with life juices that had sprayed his face and head. Her heart heavy, Jessie dismounted and tethered her horse to a section of fence as Ki pulled up behind her. She raced to Bruce Southerland, whom she'd always called Mr. Southerland, out of respect. If she had never known her real father, Bruce Southerland was the kind of man she would have wanted as a father. Strong. Proud. Tough. Compassionate. With a heart as big as the sky. She knelt beside the dying man, who twisted his head to look up at her, then grimaced in agony.

"J-Jessie . . ."

This was no time for questions, for accusations, for saying things like, Why didn't you contact me earlier if you knew they were getting out of prison and maybe heading here? We could've been here and done something. But even in his dying moment, Bruce Southerland must've read her wondering and torn expression.

"I'm . . . sorry . . . should've wired you earlier . . . pride . . . damn fool pride. I thought I could handle it . . . thought there'd only be three . . . but there were ten of them . . ."

Jessie held his head in her hands, choking back on her tears of pain and rage.

"Ten?" Ki breathed, kneeling beside Jessie. "They must have planned a rendezvous with a few former gang members before they got out."

"You . . . always been like a daughter to me, Jess . . . I know you won't let . . . this go unavenged . . ."

"I'm going to find them, Mr. Southerland. They'll pay with their lives. You have my word."

He chuckled, a bitter sound. "Bastards . . . didn't hear 'em ride up . . . We were eating . . . They. . . . walked right in . . . shot me . . . six, seven times . . . Thought I was dead, they did . . . I couldn't move . . . drifting in and out . . . Listened to 'em . . ." A tear squeezed from his eye. "My wife . . . raped her . . . shot my boys dead . . . left 'em . . . inside to burn . . . with our home . . ."

The heat from the crackling flames covered Jessie's expression of cold fury in a sheen of sweat.

"Throw me . . . in the fire, Jess . . . with my family . . . Promise me . . . Only fitting . . . bury the old guy with his family . . . They rode . . . half hour ago . . . away . . . south . . . They're evil men . . . not fit to live . . ."

And Bruce Southerland died, his last breath a rasping death gurgle. Jessie stayed kneeling beside him for what felt to her like an eternity. A tear broke from the corner of her eye. She clenched her jaw. She brushed shut the eyes of Mr. Southerland.

"Ki . . . I can't do it. You . . . you do what he asked."

She stood and walked back to her horse. Behind her, Ki carried the body of Bruce Southerland in his arms as close to the fire as possible, then pitched the body into the flames.

"Jessie, are you all right?"

7

She noticed she was trembling. She felt light-headed from grief and cold murderous fury. She turned and stared Ki dead in the eye.

"He said they left a half hour ago, riding south," Jessie said, then mounted her gelding. "I want them, Ki. I want them dead like nobody I've ever wanted dead in my life. Mr. Southerland was right. They aren't fit to live. He was too good a man to have died this way, to have watched his family . . ." She couldn't finish getting the words out; they seemed like something fiery and living in her throat.

Ki nodded. "I understand. Let's ride."

And they rode away from that funeral pyre without looking back.

Jessie kept her stare fixed on the far-reaching sweep of the plain to the south, her jaw set with grim determination, her heart burning with vengeance.

Behind Jessie and Ki, three buzzards circled the inferno that had been the Southerland ranch.

Jessie caught the faint sounds of grim-sounding laughter in the distance. She looked at Ki, who had been eyeing the hoofprints in the hard-packed soil for several miles. The sounds of laughter came from the hills, maybe a hundred yards south. They couldn't see the outlaws, but they could hear them. It sounded like they were celebrating. Jessie felt her blood boil with vengeance. She looked at Ki, who nodded and slid his Winchester from the scabbard.

They closed on the hills, scouring the ridges for any sign of an outlaw, but found no one.

They dismounted, tethered their mounts to brush, then began swiftly, silently climbing a gully. The closer they came to the top of the hill, the louder the voices grew. Jessie checked the terrain. In spots, the hill was a lacework of deep gullies that seemed to have been carved into the side of the hill by some supernatural force. Ahead, the ground leveled out, and she saw some boulders behind which they could take cover.

"Damn, Priestley, I knew you'd come through for ol' Judd Grimm. Didn't spend nary a gold ingot of this while we was in—I hope. I'll remember ya—I think. After I count it."

"Told ya we'd wait, Judd. Damn bastards we got earlier, they deserved this day of reckoning. Jist too bad we can't do the whole damn town."

"Who the hell says we might not yet?"

Some laughter.

" 'Sides, me and my brother, we laid the groundwork for that mining company job while we was in. Reason I didn't tell ya 'bout it sooner . . ." Laughter. "Well, I think ya unnerstand, first day out, I don't need to be chasin' my boys into Mexico to get my cut."

Jessie, her adrenaline racing, her heart pounding in her ears, unholstered her revolver. As they topped the ridge, Jessie and Ki crouched behind a boulder. They listened.

"Nah, I've changed my mind about Goodwill anyways. We took care of the biggest bastard, Mr. Jury Foreman hisself. Some of those cowpokes we cut down, I recognized them from a few years ago. We've done enough reckoning for one day. We laid down a nice little hangman's

9

trail. Somebody'll surely find them swinging by the neck by the creek, know they escaped the judgment day of ol' Judd Grimm and his gang. What we do now, we head down into Mexico. Knowed me a big-shot Mex general there. Bribe him with a few of these ingots, he'll let us lay low. Course now, we'll have to stash the rest somewhere, safe from greedy greasy Mex hands, ya unnerstand."

The outlaws laughed.

With her .38 Colt, Jessie drew aim on a big outlaw standing over a trunk filled with a glittering cache of gold ingots. She assumed he was Judd Grimm, since he was doing all the talking and planning and most of the laughing. And she determined he was going to die laughing over his gold.

Then, as chance would have it, one of the outlaws looked up and spotted Jessie as sunlight glinted off her gun.

Yelling and scrambling, the outlaws grabbed for iron.

★

Chapter 2

A lead beehive instantly swarmed over their position. Jessie and Ki ducked as bullets whined off stone all around them. They had no chance to return fire, at least not right away. Vengeance had blinded Jessie; she should've moved with more caution, more wariness, but now, she knew, was no time for second guessing.

They were both fighting for their lives.

The outlaws were maybe forty feet below Jessie and Ki, grouped in a shallow bowl at the base of the hill. They were all long-haired, bearded men in denim and wide-crowned Stetsons. And they were quick on the draw, stood their ground, defying death, fanning revolvers and jacking repeater rifles as quick as lightning.

"Priestley, get that fuckin' gold strapped on!"

Jessie and Ki spread out, staying crouched behind a line of boulders as slugs ricocheted off rock. Her eyelids slitted against stone chips spraying her face, Jessie popped up over a boulder and drilled the outlaw she assumed was Priestley in the forehead with one deadly accurate .38 slug.

11

Judd Grimm howled a vicious oath as Priestley collapsed beneath a shower of blood and muck over the cache of gold. Outlaws, scrambling to mount whinnying, bucking horses, kept firing wildly up the hill.

Ki fired away with his Winchester, as he braved the whining lead storm, weaving and bobbing down the line of boulders, his face savage with determination.

"Get the goddamn gold! Screw him, he's dead!"

Ki pumped a round into the chest of another outlaw as the vermin tried to heft the trunk onto a pack horse. The outlaw spun and toppled into the sheet of dust whiplashing around the scrambling gunmen.

And then there were eight.

And gold glittered in the sunlight as it spilled all over the ground.

Jessie was forced to hunch behind a boulder as sizzling lead kept hacking off bits and hunks of stone near her face. She looked up and glimpsed something long and narrow twirling through the air. It was flying in Ki's direction. It was sizzling.

Dynamite!

"Ki!" she screamed. "Run!"

Ki's eyes widened as the dynamite stick plunked to the ground beside him. The fuse had sparked down to a quarter inch and was vanishing quickly.

Ki bolted, as lead tracked him and screeched off rock.

The stick blew.

And Jessie watched in horror and anguish as Ki disappeared behind a cloud of smoke and fire.

He tumbled down the side of the hill, end over end. It felt to Ki as if he would never stop falling. His ears rang and the sky spun, and the sounds of gunfire and cursing and pounding hooves seemed miles away. It was a steep tumble, and he couldn't stop himself from falling. He saw stars explode in his eyes as his skull banged off rock and objects speared him in the ribs, driving the wind from his lungs.

Finally, he rolled up in a heap. For what felt like an eternity, he lay there, unmoving, a throbbing roar in his ears. He tasted the blood in his mouth; grit and sweat stung his eyes, blurred his vision. Nothing looked or felt real to him for long, terrible moments.

At least, he thought, he was alive.

Then he heard it.

Distant at first. Then growing, a soft tambourinelike sound. Finally, a noise that shattered his senses as the din of weapons fire and thundering hooves faded.

Cold fear tore through Ki's heart. His vision cleared, and he found it staring him right in the eye.

It was the biggest diamondback rattlesnake he had ever seen. Its fat, coiled body seemed to glisten in the fierce sunlight as the diamondback loomed over him, less than five feet away from his face. Its forked tongue flickered in and out; its fangs were long and curved and dripping with venom. Black, lifeless eyes stared right at Ki. If the snake bit him now, in his weakened, dazed state, he knew he might well die within minutes.

The diamondback coiled tighter and shuddered even higher, a shimmering demonic apparition in Ki's partly blurred sight.

Slowly, carefully, his heart pounding in his ears, Ki fisted his hand around the hilt of his sword. He would get one chance, and if he missed . . .

Buzzard meat.

The fat shovel head of the serpent leaned back an inch, and its lethal maw opened even wider. It was ready to bite, sink its venomous fangs into flesh.

With all the strength and speed he could command in an eye blink, Ki whipped his sword free from its scabbard as the serpent lunged for his face. Whipping his legs sideways, thrusting the blade around, Ki sliced the serpent's head off with one stroke of his sword, a blur that left in its wake a pod-burst of muck. The fat, headless body writhed in death throes at Ki's feet as he stood.

Then he heard another rattler. He whirled and found two more serpents. They were racing at him. He had landed in a viper's nest!

He had started to swing the sword for another decapitating blow, hoping he had enough time to kill the first rattler then the second, when two shots rang out and two fat shovel-headed demons were blown across the gorge in gory reptilian tatters.

Light-headed, ears ringing, Ki could barely make out Jessie's voice as she called his name. He wobbled on rubbery legs and felt the warm stickiness of his own blood trickling down his face and neck. The fall had busted him up good, he knew.

He managed a step up the hill, saw Jessie, fading

in and out, then collapsed as the world turned black.

Jessie was worried sick about Ki.

She had dragged him a dozen feet up the gully, and into the shade. She had found no more rattlers.

The human vipers had fled the area more than an hour ago.

Jessie sat on a flat rock, watching Ki, concerned and afraid. His chest rose and fell, his breathing sounded even, his pulse was steady, and she'd checked and found no broken bones she could see. But he was out cold. There were deep gashes in his skull, which she had cleaned with tepid water from her canteen. She was not a doctor, though she'd done some caretaking in her time, and if Ki didn't come around soon, she'd have to lash him to his horse and ride to Goodwill in search of a sawbones. She had already brought their mounts into the gully, ready to ride at a moment's notice if her fear for Ki's condition deepened. The dynamite blast had literally, she reflected, hurled Ki off the hill. Had he hesitated, had he been perhaps three or four feet closer to the blast . . . She shuddered, unable to think of what could have happened.

It was terrible and terrifying for her to see Ki like this. Here was a man, her friend, her bodyguard, her mentor, who had faced down death countless times, who could deal out and take punches as hard as a mule's kick, now unconscious and unmoving and possibly near the brink of death. She felt helpless and alone.

She gently washed Ki's face with water. She decided she would give it another thirty minutes; then she would take Ki to Goodwill.

She didn't have to wait that long.

Ki's eyelids fluttered open. "J-Jessie . . . how . . ." He groaned.

"Easy, Ki. Don't try to stand. Just lie there."

"How long have I been out?"

"Close . . . almost two hours now."

Ki groaned, sat up. "We have to get going. They're getting away . . ."

"You're in no shape to ride, Ki. I think I should take you to Goodwill and find a doctor."

But Ki proved himself as stubborn as ever. He stood, but wobbled, and Jessie bolted to her feet, fearing Ki would topple over. She put her hands on his shoulders to steady him.

"We're going, Jessie. That's final. They damn near killed me. I get very upset when someone tries to blow me up into a thousand pieces with dynamite."

"I feel responsible, Ki. I can't let you ride."

"Why do you feel responsible? You saved my life. I wouldn't have seen that dynamite if you hadn't warned me."

"I let my heart control me. I was in a blind rage. I bulled right into the situation."

"It's not your fault. Look, I feel fine."

"Come on, Ki. I know you. You're as stubborn as a mule. Truthfully, how do you feel?"

Ki sucked in a deep breath, some of the fire fading from his determined gaze. "Weak. Sick. My ears are still ringing. But I can shake it off."

Jessie knew that if any man could put his personal physical pain aside it was Ki. And she could tell he was not going to relent.

"All right. All right, but if it looks to me like you can't ride, I'm finding a doctor. Fair enough?"

A ghost of a smile danced over Ki's lips. He nodded and said, "Fair enough. Now let's get out of here. We've malingered long enough."

But Ki knew he was hurting. As he rode beside Jessie across the barren, baking plain, it was all he could do to stay upright in the saddle. He was dizzy and nauseated, but the ringing in his ears was fading. He fought for balance, willing the pain away. He had to put up a strong front or he knew Jessie would stop right there in the middle of the plain and force him to go to a doctor. He couldn't let that happen. He knew how important catching up to the Grimm gang was to her. It was important to him, too; it was personal for both of them. If he got his hands around Judd Grimm's throat, he'd ram a stick of lit dynamite down the outlaw's gullet and savor his vengeance.

"How do you feel, Ki?"

"Fine."

"You sure?"

"I'm fine."

He checked the ground. Fresh horse droppings were strung along the hard-packed earth. The Grimm brothers were not that far ahead.

"This is bad country where we're headed, Jessie. Bandits, renegade Apaches and Yaquis. If we're forced to go into Mexico . . . well, I hope somebody somewhere is smiling down on us."

Jessie grinned. "I know you're not telling me you want to head back, so what's your point?"

17

"Fear—for you. I'd hate like hell to see anything happen to you. I can never help feeling that way. I'm your bodyguard, remember?"

"I can hold my own, Ki."

And he knew she could. This woman's toughness, her grittiness, her determination never failed to amaze Ki. And often, as now, he felt inspired by Jessie.

The sun was beginning to sink for the jagged hills to the west when a long line of men on horseback suddenly appeared on the horizon. They were coming in from the west, riding at a trot, with the sun to their backs.

And they were heading straight for Jessie and Ki.

"A posse?" Jessie wondered aloud, as they halted their mounts, and waited.

"Too many for a posse." At a hundred yards, Ki recognized the blue uniforms and white hats of U.S. soldiers.

A boiling wall of dust followed the soldiers, as sunlight glinted off buttons and sabers.

"There must be between fifty and a hundred of them," Jessie said. "This isn't good, Ki. This looks like trouble."

The line of riders pulled up in front of Jessie and Ki. Not all of the men wore uniforms, Ki saw. A dozen men dressed in denim, with revolvers and repeater rifles and large hunting knives sheathed in leather on their hips, sat on the left flank of the soldiers.

A tall, lean soldier guided his black gelding several feet away from the large group. He had a thick black beard, a sun-burnished face, and eyes that were hard and as black as coal.

"I'm Captain James Frederick, United States Army, First Cavalry out of Fort Mason," he announced. "We've been following a trail of dead men the whole day. We're tired and angry and on edge. I'm going to ask you this one time and one time only. Who the hell are you people and just what the hell are you doing out here?"

★

Chapter 3

First, Jessie had insisted on a private conference with Captain Frederick before answering any questions. She had gotten it. The cavalry captain from Fort Mason of the southern Arizona Territory had ordered his men to take a break and then followed Jessie and Ki on foot, with a short, squat, red-bearded Sergeant Milrose by his side, away from the soldiers and the twelve ferocious-looking civilians. Then Jessie had told the Captain exactly who the hell they were and what the hell they were doing out there.

Finally, as sweat soaked into his beard and flies buzzed around his hard-eyed, grim-faced visage, Captain Frederick nodded and scoured the faces of both Jessie and Ki. "So, you're the Lone Star legend. That's right, I've heard of both of you. Jessica Starbuck of Starbuck Enterprises and her half-American, half-Japanese bodyguard." If he was impressed, he didn't show it. Jessie studied the man's face. Out there, in the dust and the heat, he was a rugged and mean-looking soldier, but in a good-looking way, she decided. Cleaned up and shaved he would be a very handsome man, the kind of man who could make women of high society swoon. She pictured him sauntering into an upper-class society function, decked out in a clean and pressed uniform. He had presence, that certain quality called charisma, which made him a natural born leader. And he was also very tough, she could sense, a hard man with a hard job, whatever the Army's job was at the moment. She knew she was looking at a man who would not shirk his duty to his country, or be afraid to fight to the death for what he believed in. She also detected a glimmer of compassion for his fellow man somewhere in those eyes, a man who had seen his own personal suffering, a man who could be reasoned with. She also sensed he was fighting not to look at her for what she was—a stunningly beautiful woman. And she felt attracted to him. Under any other circumstances, Jessie thought a romantic interlude with the Captain might prove interesting.

The Captain tapped the hilt of his saber with a steady but impatient hand. "However, I do not need any more lone wolves out here on a vengeance hunt than I already have on my hands."

Jessie peered at the Captain. "Already have? What are you saying, Captain?"

"I'm saying this, Miss Jessie, so listen good, both of you. I have seventy soldiers here, all of them volunteers for this mission. For two weeks now we have been on a hunt for a band of renegade Apaches who have attacked and slaughtered white settlers across three territories. Some of my soldiers have lost family to these renegade Apaches, and this thing is going to turn ugly, how ugly I'm not sure. Already, we have been forced into several engagements and left behind more than a few dead Indians, not to mention losing two dozen of my own men. What we are is a hunting party; we have been sanctioned by the governors of three territories, who in turn have been officially authorized by Washington."

"Sanctioned? Authorized?" Ki queried.

Captain Frederick nodded. "Yes. To hunt down every renegade Apache, every bandit and outlaw we can, and either bring them to justice or kill them. In short, we are to clean up Texas and the New Mexico and Arizona territories, even if that means going down into Mexico and even at the risk of starting another war with the Mexicans."

"And I suppose you're telling Ki and me," Jessie said, "to pack it up and go home and forget about the Grimm gang."

"Not at all," the Captain said. "You want them, you ride with me, but under the authority of the United States Army."

"We ride alone," Ki said.

"Not this time."

And Captain Frederick held his ground.

The Captain, standing tall and straight, eyelids cracked to mere slits under the blazing sun, forged on. "Understand, I do not need either to be looking over my shoulder for any more renegade vengeance hunters, or looking ahead with my scouts only to find you carved up on the desert floor for the buzzards and the coyotes. I take this mission seriously, deadly seriously. I am taking complete and full control of your person as of this moment. I am responsible for the lives of my men and for the lives of any and all Americans I come across. I do not want innocent blood on my hands if I can help it. Presently, you might be considered innocent blood. After all, there are only two of you."

Jessie knew they had no choice, and told Ki as much. She looked at the group of soldiers, who were eating cold beans and drinking from canteens and feeding their mounts. She noticed that the civilians had managed to sidle away from the soldiers and were nearby, watching and eavesdropping.

"Who are they?" Jessie asked, nodding at the civilians.

"Bounty hunters," Sergeant Milrose put in with distaste in his voice and look.

"Jake Kingston, ma'am," the biggest and broadest and meanest-looking bounty hunter called out. "Cap'n picked us up yesterday, offered us the same deal—or he threatened to take our guns away from us. Not very gentlemanly of him, I might add. But, what the hell, we're here, and crossing the Rio Grande is fine with us. We go south of the border, well, me and the boys are here for some Injun scalps, too, and if we kill us a few greaseball bandits along the way, I'll hang a few Mex scalps from my saddle, too. Cap'n's got a job for the government; all we want is some money. Cold hard cash, and blood money is always the best."

Several of the bounty hunters laughed.

Captain Frederick shook his head in disgust. "Kingston and his men are veterans of the War

Between the States. Fought under the Confederate flag."

"You make that sound like something dirty, Cap'n," a bounty hunter called out. "Like we's somethin' you might step in."

Frederick ignored them. "So, you can see what you'll be riding with. The U.S. Army, and a dozen men of questionable character and reputation, bounty hunters with a thirst for blood money and maybe more than just a little hate and prejudice in their hearts. Well? You ride with us? Or . . . well, the town of Goodwill's a half day's ride north."

"You already have our answer," Jessie said.

"Then let's saddle up," a bounty hunter called out in a contemptuous voice. "Time's wastin'."

"I get the distinct and bad impression, Captain," Jessie said, "that there's some serious conflict of interests here. What I want to know—no, what I'm going to insist on is that we get Judd Grimm and his bunch. It's personal, I told you; they murdered a good friend of my father's, slaughtered his whole family and burned his ranch."

"I don't care how it gets done, or who gets who, as long as it gets done. I'm not after Grimm anyway, but if he shows up somewhere along the way . . ."

"Then it's first come first serve," Jake Kingston interrupted. "Falo, you got any paper on some of the Grimm gang?"

"Yeah, now that you mention it." Jessie watched in rising anger as she saw a bounty hunter with a hump on his back dig wanted posters out of his saddlebag. "Yeah, Jake, there's a Peters, Marlowe, Judsen, and Thomas, all Grimm gang boys. Ten big ones altogether."

Jake Kingston grinned at Jessie. "Like I said, lady. First come first serve."

Jessie said nothing, but thought, We'll see.

Captain Frederick cleared his throat, glared at Kingston, then told Jessie, "We're after an Apache named Cochillo Apono, a renegade chief with a band of about a hundred bucks."

"White man calls Cochillo 'Red Ghost.'" Kingston chuckled. "Seems he can slip into a camp in the middle of the night and cut every throat around without making the first bit of noise. Then disappears. Moves like the wind."

Jessie had heard of Red Ghost. She knew what the bounty hunter said was true: Cochillo Apono was an Apache who had put pure terror in the hearts of white settlers in the New Mexico and Arizona territories.

Ki spoke up. "Jessie, I need to talk with you a minute. Over here."

Captain Frederick scowled. "I'll wait with my men. You have two minutes."

Ki led Jessie farther away from the hunting party. "I don't like it, Jessie. The last time I heard, America was a free country and people were allowed to go where they wanted. I think it's a mistake to ride with these men."

"But if they're heading in the same direction we are, Ki, we don't need to be getting caught up in their cross fire. This Captain Frederick will make things hard on us if we don't cooperate. You heard him: He's been sanctioned by the United States

25

Government. I don't like it when someone else holds all the cards either, believe me. But let's work with him on this."

Ki seemed to think long and hard about what Jessie had said; then finally he nodded.

Jessie and Ki returned to their mounts. She felt the eyes of the bounty hunters crawling all over her.

"Nice to have you along on this little trip, ma'am. Zeke Zebulon, at your service. Need anything, anything at all, don't hesitate to call on me."

She looked at the bounty hunter with the lopsided grin showing a set of crooked, tobacco-stained teeth. He had a narrow face and laughing eyes, a wad of chaw packed in his mouth. Zeke Zebulon launched a stream of brown juice through the air. Several bounty hunters chuckled as Jessie snorted, coldly looked away from Zeke Zebulon, and mounted her gelding.

"Awright, boys," Jake Kingston said. "Rein it in. We're about business. Pleasure can wait."

Ki ran a hard-eyed stare over the bounty hunters as Captain Frederick ordered his men to mount up. The bounty hunters returned Ki's look with eyes full of contempt and challenge. Jessie sensed violence on the verge of exploding, but it didn't, as Ki mounted. The bounty hunters were trouble, she thought. Vicious violent men who loved only money. Blood money.

As they rode along, Jessie discovered just how much of a plague riding with the bounty hunters would be.

She and Ki rode beside Captain Frederick across a vast stretch of baking hard-packed plain, Jessie saw blood suddenly trickle down the side of Ki's face. Ki wiped the blood away. The Captain noticed Ki's condition and scoured his punished features with concern that didn't escape Jessie.

"What happened to you?"

"Judd Grimm tried to blow me off the side of a hill with some dynamite," Ki answered.

From several horses down on the left flank, Jake Kingston chuckled. "Dynamite, huh? Well, you see those three packhorses to your right?"

Both Jessie and Ki looked to the right flank and found three packhorses, each one laden with two crates marked U.S. ARMY.

"There's enough dynamite in those crates to wipe out half the population of Mexico," Kingston said, grinning. "Say that evens the odds a little. 'Course, don't wanna see nobody here use a few sticks on my paying-paper catch. I need something in one piece to take back and collect the bounty."

The more he talked, the more Jessie despised Jake Kingston. She ignored the bounty hunters, who would frequently cast a roving lust-filled eye her way.

"In case you were wondering," Captain Frederick suddenly said, "we're heading for the Rio Grande. The U.S. Government is fed up with outlaws who will commit the most heinous of crimes and then flee for the sanctuary of Mexico."

"So, it's always been your intention to go into Mexico," Ki commented, but drew no response from the Captain.

"Judd Grimm said he was going into Mexico," Jessie said. "We overheard him mention something about a general down there who would give him a place to hide."

Captain Frederick nodded. "That would be General Paco Alfredo of the federales. I've heard of him. The report on him is that he's corrupt and he's headquartered in a town called San Pedro, rules the place with an iron fist and a bunch of brutal soldiers who stay drunk on pulque most of the time—when they aren't raping civilian women. That's where all the outlaws head; even renegade Apaches and Yaquis have been known to head there. I don't think I have to tell you it's a bad place. It could just be we might have to march right into San Pedro and demand the general hand over any and all outlaws . . . or else . . ."

"And Grimm's got a trunk full of gold to buy a safe haven," Ki added.

Captain Frederick shook his head, looking disgusted. "So the general would do all he could to make sure Grimm stays safe and sound and under his care."

"That gold, that would be the Coleman Mining Company out of Colorado," Zeke Zebulon said, and chuckled. "The payroll was ripped off about three weeks ago. Rumor was Grimm planned the heist from inside."

"That gold belong to anybody that can get their hands on it first, Cap'n?" a bounty hunter asked.

"It belongs to the United States, mister," Frederick shot back. "Namely the Coleman Colorado Mining Company."

The bounty hunter cursed.

They rode in silence, but the clop of countless hooves, the creaking of leather, the horses' whickering, and the buzzing of flies filled Jessie's ears with a constant deafening noise. She was glad to be riding in the front, because the soldiers picking up the rear were forced to eat clouds of dust.

They saw them suddenly in the distance. There were six of them, riding slowly out of the shimmering heat mist.

"Injuns," Zeke Zebulon said.

They rode bareback, and as the six Indians, dressed only in breechcloths and toting war clubs, lances, and bows, became clearly visible at a hundred feet, Captain Frederick held up his hand and ordered everyone to stop.

"Red Ghost always rides a white stallion," the Captain said. "I don't see any white stallion. I want to talk to them," he added, holding up his hand in greeting to the Indians.

"They Apaches," a bounty hunter spat. "Mark my word, this area is crawlin' with Red Ghost's bunch, since they spilled over here from New Mexico."

"Let's take 'em, fellas. They fair game."

Jessie snapped her head sideways and saw the bounty hunters slide Winchester repeater rifles from their scabbards. Before the Captain could say anything, the bounty hunters were firing their rifles at the Indians.

"You men! Stop this second!" the Captain roared. "I order you to stop firing!"

It was too late. The bounty hunters had broken from the ranks and were jacking levers on their rifles and drilling the startled Indians where they sat. Indians toppled to the ground, spurting blood from bullet-riddled chests. Jessie was amazed at the speed, the daring, and the lethal marksmanship of the bounty hunters.

"Move out!" the Captain bellowed, and the cavalry thundered ahead.

One Indian had escaped the lightning assault and was riding at breakneck speed across the plain, disappearing into the shimmering heat.

Jessie watched in disgust as the bounty hunters descended on the dead Indians with flashing steel. They began scalping the bodies. They were like animals, Jessie thought.

"They Apache, awright." Zeke Zebulon laughed. "Seen enough Apaches in my day to knowed one."

Captain Frederick drew his Starr Double-Action Army .44 and cracked the air with three quick rounds, firing over the heads of the bounty hunters. And the bounty hunters stopped their savaging of the corpses.

Jake Kingston stood, a bloody scalp in his hand, as Captain Frederick swung his aim toward the leader of the bounty hunters.

"You draw that piece on me, Cap'n," Kingston rasped, "you best be prepared to use it."

Captain Frederick cocked the hammer on his revolver, a chilling sound in the tense silence. "I am."

★

Chapter 4

Judging from the look in the cavalry captain's eyes, Jessie had no doubt that he would gun down Jake Kingston where he stood and leave him for the buzzards. And she wouldn't blame the Captain if he did just that. The sight of what the bounty hunters had done to the dead Indians sickened her. Jessie draped her hand over the butt of her revolver, in case the bounty hunters decided to do something crazy.

And crazy would be throwing themselves into a gunfight with seventy soldiers, all of whom had followed their captain's lead and drawn revolvers or unsheathed rifles from saddle scabbards.

Jake Kingston ran a cold eye over the array of weapons leveled on them. Then, finally, he nodded and chuckled. "I'll remember this, Cap'n."

"See that you do," the Captain said. "Now get on your horses. You're just damn lucky. You just be damn grateful, mister, I don't take your weapons right now and send you on your way."

"I thought it was first come, first serve, Cap'n," Zeke Zebulon growled. "Thought you said you didn't care who got who."

"I also said I wanted to talk to these Apaches."

"And ask 'em what?" Kingston said. "Where is Red Ghost? Anyways, we didn't hear ya say that."

"That's most peculiar," the Captain said. "All of a sudden you go deaf, when earlier you overheard my conversation with these two from fifty feet away. Get on your horses."

As the bounty hunters, with their gory trophies in hand, mounted up, Sergeant Milrose muttered in an acid voice, "Damn scum. Why don't you just send them on their way, sir? They disobeyed a direct order."

"We might need all the manpower we can get when we cross the border, Sergeant, that's why. Even them. Hey!" Captain Frederick barked at the bounty hunters. "As sure as I'm sitting here, you disobey another order, I don't give a damn if you hear it or not, you won't get another chance. Understood?"

"Yeah, we understand, awright, Cap'n, sir," Jake Kingston said, and threw a mock salute at the Captain.

Jessie detected a note of cunning in Kingston's voice. Given the savagery she'd just seen, she trusted the bounty hunters even less now. She looked at Ki, who looked ready to shoot the bounty hunters himself. Ki returned her look with contempt and dismay over the spectacle he had just witnessed.

"I would say you certainly have your hands full, Captain," Jessie said. "Believe me when I tell you,

32

if you have any more trouble out of that bunch, Ki and I are right behind you."

"I hope you being along, ma'am, doesn't make it worse. I'd like to say a beautiful woman like you has no business out here, but something tells me you can hold your own in any situation."

"I'll take that as a compliment, Captain."

"That's the way I intended it."

It was nightfall when they made camp at the base of a long chain of jagged and ominous hills. A full moon cast the campsite in an eerie soft white glow. Soldiers moved to secure the perimeter. Captain Frederick picked out his sentries and ordered his scouts into the hills to check the area for Apaches. Several camp fires were built.

Ki watched all this activity with a solemn heart. He didn't like having to ride with these soldiers, much less being forced to ride with bounty hunters who were no better than the men they hunted. He was disgusted with the situation, but he knew Jessie was right, that they had no choice. Ride with the Army or go home to the ranch. Captain Frederick was in charge, and he had the final word since he was empowered by the United States Government to do whatever it took to bring fugitives in three territories to justice.

"How are you feeling, Ki?"

Ki looked at Jessie as she sat down on her bedroll, sipped water from her canteen, then began eating a biscuit and cold beans.

"I'm all right, Jessie."

"You look like you're in deep thought. Can I ask what you're thinking?"

"That I wish we had other options."

"I second that."

Jessie followed Ki's stare toward the bounty hunters. They were grouped by themselves near the edge of the campsite. Several of the hunters were swilling from whiskey bottles, smoking cigars, and talking among themselves.

"I don't like the feeling I'm getting from over there," Ki said. "Something smells, and it's not the trail grit. They're plotting something."

"They can't do anything. The Captain's posted a dozen sentries around the entire perimeter." Jessie cracked a grin. "Not even Red Ghost could slip in here tonight."

"I wouldn't be so sure about that. One of those Apaches got away, and if Red Ghost is in the area, he might just want to teach these bluebellies a lesson. No thanks to our friends, the bounty hunters."

"I suggest you two get a good night's sleep."

Jessie and Ki looked up at the tall, broad shadow that was Captain Frederick.

"We'll be moving out just before dawn. We should be crossing the border by midday tomorrow." The Captain stayed there for a long moment. And Ki could sense he was looking at Jessie in a fond way that betrayed his desire for her. "Good night," he said, and moved off.

"He seems like a good man," Jessie said.

"And you seem like a good woman in his eyes," Ki commented, then showed Jessie a wry grin.

"Get some sleep, Ki. I won't be sneaking off with the Captain. It would be bad for morale."

"There's enough bad morale around here for three armies."

Jessie grunted, finished her biscuit and beans, then lay down in her bedroll.

Ki had trouble falling asleep. He lay there, staring up at the sky, the full moon, listening to the soft drone of conversations and the crackle of flames around him. Gut instinct warned him that there would be trouble before the night was over.

Ki didn't have to wait long.

He finally fell asleep, but he was abruptly awakened by the chaos of shouting and cursing and gunfire.

Ki and Jessie bolted to their feet, guns in hand. Soldiers were scrambling pell-mell all over the campsite, firing into the night.

Shooting at nothing that Ki could see.

Jessie ran up to Captain Frederick, who was screaming at Sergeant Milrose.

"Captain, what's happening?" Jessie demanded.

"The sky fell, that's what happened!"

"Where are you, you bastards!" a soldier was hollering into the darkness.

"How could this have happened?" another soldier cried.

"You should've been watching your post!" another soldier berated a shamefaced bluecoat.

Jessie and Ki followed the Captain toward three outstretched bodies. They were soldiers. Their throats had been cut from ear to ear, and they had been scalped.

"Sir, all the sentries have had their throats cut!" a soldier reported to the Captain. "Bastards even scalped them!"

"Damn it!"

"And the bounty hunters, sir, they're gone. They took the dynamite!"

Captain Frederick swore viciously, then shouted for his men to stop firing as they couldn't see a damn thing out there to shoot at.

"Those bounty hunters, they couldn't have killed our men like that!" Sergeant Milrose said.

"Red Ghost," the Captain muttered, as the shots echoed off into the hills. "When I catch up to Kingston and his pack, I'm placing them under arrest."

"Well, I'm sure you're bound to find them in San Pedro, Captain," Jessie said.

"Maybe Red Ghost will get them first," Ki said to no one in particular.

A soldier walked up to Captain Frederick. He looked sheepish, and blood trickled down the side of his face. "I'm sorry, sir, Lieutenant Connors and I . . . They took us by surprise . . . hit us over the head . . . took the packhorses. I don't see how they could have gotten out of here with no one hearing them."

"Probably the same time Red Ghost crept in here and was cutting throats and collecting scalps," the Captain growled. "You were lucky, soldier, that a knock on the head was all you got."

Then they heard it. Everyone froze, staring up at the hills. It sounded like the howl of a coyote or a wolf. The chilling cry went on and on for what seemed like an eternity.

"What is it?" a soldier asked.

"Shut up!" Captain Frederick ordered, peering

off into the night, as the eerie sound kept washing down over the campsite.

Ki spotted the lone figure, high up on the hill. As the shadowy Apache stood beneath the light of the full moon, there was no mistaking the lance he held up in a gesture of triumph. And in his other hand he held the scalps of the soldiers he had killed. With a gesture that looked like contempt, he flung the scalps away from him. Then Red Ghost vanished just as soldiers began peppering the ridge with gunfire.

"Hold your fire!"

Captain Frederick had to repeat the order until every gun fell silent. "I want two dozen men saddled up to move out now. I'll be damned if I'll stand by," he told Jessie and Ki, "and bury my men without going into those hills after Red Ghost."

But Ki knew the Captain would find no sign of Red Ghost.

The Captain had come back into camp without finding the first trace of Red Ghost. Even a full hour after returning from his futile venture into the hills, he was still enraged and still cursing every living thing under the moon. They buried their own right where they had died. Jessie didn't think that was normal Army procedure. She would have figured they'd send the bodies back to Fort Mason for a military burial. Then again, there was nothing normal about the Captain's mission.

The rest of the night there was no sight or sound of Red Ghost. It was as if the Apache chief had vanished into thin air. No one slept.

And Jessie kept vigil, not trusting the soldiers to keep the campsite secure from deadly invaders.

When the first rays of dawn broke across the sky, the cavalry was saddled up and ready to head out for the border. Jessie could sense the tension, the hatred, the violence poised to erupt. An Apache had slipped into the campsite, killed their own without making a sound, and vanished into the night, only to stand on a hill and taunt them before disappearing into the wilderness altogether. No one spoke; no one ate or even drank coffee. The soldiers looked grim and determined.

It was mid-morning when the Santiago Mountains loomed to the south. Captain Frederick ordered the march to a halt and sent scouts ahead to look for Apaches and to find a way through the wall of rock.

"Why don't we just go around the mountains, Captain?" Jessie asked. "It would seem a safer and far wiser course then taking a chance of getting trapped in a gorge."

"Safer, maybe, but I've never played it safe, Miss Jessie. Besides, going around, it will take too long, maybe burn up a whole half day," he answered. "And if there are any of Red Ghost's brothers in the mountains, then let's just say I want to bring them down out of those mountains."

Jessie didn't agree with the Captain's thinking. He was becoming bullheaded and driven by vengeance, but then again, she couldn't criticize him for that. They waited for the scouts to return. An hour later the scouts reported to the Captain that there were no signs of any Apaches in the hills, but there were fresh horse droppings that led through a gorge.

The hunting party moved out.

Jessie tensed as they began riding through the gorge. She looked up the steep walls of rock and saw nothing but boulders and brush. Still, she knew an enemy could be hiding above them, somewhere in a lacework of gullies that cut the sides of the mountain.

They were halfway through the gorge when Jessie's suspicions were proven right.

Shots rang out from above the hunting party. Two soldiers, blood and brain matter spraying from their shattered skulls, tumbled from their horses. Then all hell descended on the gorge.

Jessie couldn't see who was shooting at them, because they were only darting shadows above. The soldiers returned fire for only a few seconds, as Jessie and Ki dismounted to take cover.

Then explosions began ripping through the ranks of the soldiers, and both sides of the gorge seemed to blast apart in huge fiery clouds. They were trapped, Jessie knew. Shouts of "dynamite" and "take cover" from the soldiers were drowned by the constant barrage of explosions and gunfire raining down on them from the invisible enemy. Grimm or the bounty hunters? Jessie briefly wondered, since both the outlaws and the bounty hunters had dynamite. It didn't matter who had ambushed them at that moment. Men were dying everywhere.

Soldiers tumbled from horses as big chunks of debris slammed into them. Side by side, Jessie and Ki dashed for the cover of a gully.

"In there, Jessie!" Ki shouted, taking her by the arm as an explosion rang out right over them.

Then Jessie felt herself hurled to the ground. She looked back, realizing with fear that Ki had just shoved her away from a shower of rocks.

She saw Ki lying on the floor of the gorge, outstretched and unmoving.

★

Chapter 5

It seemed to take a tremendous effort, but Ki finally opened his eyes. His vision was blurry at first; then his sight cleared up and he found himself in a strange room. He had no idea where he was.

Or who the beautiful dark-haired woman in the white dress was who was standing over him.

Ki groaned, tried to sit up, but the woman put a hand on his bare shoulder and gently eased him back on the pillow. "Who . . . what . . . Where's Jessie?"

"Sssh. Quiet. You'll wake everyone up."

Ki stared up at the woman, confused and amazed. She had a voluptuous body, full-figured, with big cone-shaped breasts and a well-rounded rump, and she had the most strikingly beautiful face and the darkest eyes Ki had ever seen. If he hadn't ached so bad and been so worried about where he was and where Jessie was, he would've joked that he'd died and gone to heaven. The last thing he remembered was the ambush in the gorge and scrambling to throw Jessie away from rock that was plummeting straight for her head, a shower of debris that could have killed her.

Ki took a moment to look around the room. He was stretched out beneath a blanket, and he realized he was naked, as he spotted his clothing and weapons piled in the corner of the room. Still stunned and wondering if he was dreaming, he looked up at the woman, her face soft with compassion, her eyes almost shining with warmth in the light from the kerosene lantern on the nightstand. And there was something else in her eyes. Desire. Okay, Ki thought, maybe I have died and gone to heaven.

"My name is Pamela Stinson. Your friend, Jessie, she's all right, she's in the next room. We finally got her to go to sleep. She brought you here. We heard about what happened with the soldiers in the gorge."

"Where is this place?"

"This is our ranch. You're just south of the Santiago Mountains. I live here with my three brothers and our grandfather. You're safe. We cleaned you up and bandaged your wounds. Everyone's asleep. Try not to make any noise."

Ki touched his head, felt the bandage wrapped around his skull. "What time is it?"

"It's almost midnight. You've been unconscious all day. Your friend said you saved her life. She is your friend, right? I mean . . ."

"We're not involved that way. I'm her bodyguard."

"Yes. We've heard of the Starbuck name. Your name is Ki. The two of you are something of a legend in Texas. I must say . . . I'm impressed. You look quite the man."

Suddenly, without warning, she bent over and kissed Ki on the mouth. He couldn't believe it. He didn't know this woman, had just laid eyes on her, and she was breathing fire into him. He hurt and he was sore and he wasn't up for this.

Then, as she kept kissing him with her hot, moist mouth, he found that he was, indeed, up for the moment.

She pulled back and smiled shyly. "I'm not any whore . . . It's just . . . I lost my own husband about two years ago . . . He was killed by some cattle rustlers. I haven't had a man since then. And I look at you . . . I see all man. I can't help myself. And, besides, there's nothing better to cure what ails you than what I have in mind."

Jessie was safe, Ki thought. And he was alive. So why not let this beautiful woman cure what ailed him? he decided. After so many close brushes with death lately, he figured he deserved to live a little. So seize the moment, he thought. He might never get another chance for a stolen few minutes of passion the way things were going.

Pamela Stinson removed the blanket from Ki, gazed at his manhood with unconcealed hunger for a second, then hastily peeled off her dress. Her breasts were large and firm, her big nipples erect like thimbles from excitement. She lowered a breast into Ki's mouth and groaned as he gently sucked her nipple. She took his rigid member in her hand and began stroking him, teasing the head, then the shaft with probing fingers. He had to admit to himself, he was feeling much better already. She rubbed her breasts over his face. They were big, succulent, firm melons that Ki sucked on. And she smelled sweet—like honeysuckle. He was so hard he thought it would explode.

"I'm not dreaming, am I?"

She gave out a low chuckle. "No. This is real. And so's this."

Ki let out a soft groan of pleasure as she took him in her mouth, ran her lips and tongue down his shaft. Gently she squeezed his sac, kissing and licking the length of his member, her lips making soft smacking sounds as she sucked him. He cupped her breasts, kneading them, making her squirm and moan with burning passion. No, it wasn't any dream, he knew; it was all too beautifully real. She knelt up beside him on the bed, keeping him in her mouth. He ran his hand over the smooth silkiness of her buttocks, prying her cheeks open, slipping a finger into her moist and fiery hole.

Her musky smell filled him with a hunger to take her. Then she took him. She straddled him, grasping him in her hand, then sliding him into her, deep, her face twisted with a look of pleasure and pain. Gently, she rode him, sliding up and down his rock-hard manhood. She bent toward his face, kissing him, riding him, and thrusting herself down on him, faster and faster. She tried to be quiet, but she kept groaning, and Ki thought she would scream in delight and wake up the whole ranch. He spread her cheeks as she writhed, fighting to reach orgasm. Finally, her mouth locked on his mouth, she climaxed,

44

breathing a strangled cry of pure pleasure down his throat. Ki had waited long enough. With a few upward thrusts, he spurted into her, drenching her with a long, hot eruption. She collapsed on top of him.

"Oh, that was . . . that was so beautiful," she breathed into his ear. "I knew I had to have you the second I saw you. I didn't hurt you, did I?"

"I feel much better. No, I feel like a new man."

"You're going to leave in the morning, aren't you?"

"We have to."

"Oh, well, at least I'll have this moment to cherish. Maybe someday you'll return."

"Maybe."

Ki found himself getting sleepy. "I'm so tired . . ."

"Sleep then. I won't disturb you again. I'll be right here beside you."

"You're like some angel that floated down from the sky," Ki said in a weary voice. "If I'm dreaming, this is the best dream I've ever had. I'd rather not wake up."

"It's no dream. If you want me to, I can prove it again in the morning."

With a smile on his face, Ki drifted off into a deep slumber and dreamed of female angels with dark hair and hot mouths.

The next time Ki woke up, he found Jessie by his bed. Shafts of sunlight were knifing through the window across the room. Ki felt weak and sick and dizzy, but he wasn't about to tell Jessie how bad he felt.

"What time is it?" he asked.

"It's about eight o'clock. I know I'm just wasting my breath, but I think you should stay in bed. It's the second time in two days you've suffered a severe concussion."

"You're right, you're wasting your breath," Ki said, and smiled at Jessie. He sat up, trying to make the motion look as easy as possible. He kept the blanket over him.

Jessie threw him a sly grin. "I take it you feel better. Pamela Stinson proved to be quite the nurse, didn't she?"

"So, I wasn't dreaming," Ki said. "Damn. We've lost a full day, Jessie. What happened back there?"

"The Captain lost quite a few men. He's going to lose time crossing the border, having to clean up the mess we left behind back in that gorge, but I really have no idea what his plans are now. He must've lost twenty men by the looks of it. I still don't know who ambushed us."

"Why don't I get dressed, and we can thank these people and be on our way?"

"I think you already made your thanks, to at least one of our kind hosts," Jessie said, and grinned. "I'll be outside."

Outside, near the corral beyond the adobe ranch, Jessie and Ki gathered with the Stinson family. The Stinson sons were tough-looking, weathered men somewhere in their thirties. Grandfather Stinson was a lean, stoop-shouldered man with a face so weathered and heavily lined he looked a hundred years old, but he had strength and wisdom in his deep-set blue eyes. Pamela Stinson stood beside her brothers, a look of longing on her beautiful face. Jessie caught the look she cast Ki. It must've been some romp, she thought, but she was happy for Ki. After all he'd been through, she decided, he needed, no, he deserved that bit of rest and relaxation.

"Mr. Stinson, I want to thank you for all you've done," Jessie said. She offered him money, but he refused and she knew not to push the offer again. He was a proud man and he was a good man, and the Stinson sons said they were only glad they could help.

"Wish you luck, ma'am, in finding that Grimm bunch," Grandfather Stinson said. " 'Preciate you warnin' us about them. We'll keep an eye open."

Jessie and Ki mounted their horses.

"Somethin' I didn't tell you, ma'am," Grandfather Stinson said. "I know who you are, 'cause I did a piece of business involvin' some cattle with your father. This was years ago. He was a fair and honest and good man. Weren't for his help, I might never have gotten this ranch. You're as fine and as decent as he was. He'd a been real proud of his daughter."

"Thank you," Jessie said, feeling her heart ache for just a second as she remembered her father. "You've been most kind. If you ever need anything . . ."

"Don't mention it. Just be careful. These parts have become a bad place, full of outlaw vermin and renegade Apaches. We can take care of ourselves. You just get that Grimm bunch. That'll repay the favor."

They said good-bye to the Stinsons. Ki held Pamela Stinson's bittersweet gaze for a lingering moment, then smiled at the woman and touched the brim of his hat.

As they rode away from the Stinson ranch, Jessie said, "They're good people. Wouldn't you agree?"

Ki returned Jessie's knowing smile with a wry grin. "I should get knocked out saving your life more often."

They rode south across a rolling, barren sun-baked plain, heading for the Rio Grande. In the distance, a chain of jagged hills broke the terrain. Two buzzards circled over the hills.

"Something dead or dying," Ki said, watching the buzzards, his hand draped over his revolver. "Whatever it is we'll find, Jessie, it'll be more death. And more trouble. Keep your eyes open. We seem to be finding a lot of trouble lately in hills."

"You mean you're not up for another knock on the head?" Jessie cracked.

Ki chuckled. "Only if I wake up to find a dark-haired angel by my bed."

"For someone who's had a string of bad luck, you sure have seemed to come out the other side pretty good. Hey, whatever works. I'm just glad you're feeling better."

They closed on the hills. Then they heard a feeble groan, a sound that was knifed with pure misery. They dismounted near the ashes of a camp fire. Ki checked the ground.

"A lot of hoofprints. Shod. They weren't Apaches."

"Well, it was either Grimm or the bounty hunters then," Jessie said, and began climbing the gully in the direction from which the moaning came.

They found him staked out to the ground on top of the hill, spread-eagled and naked. There were signs of mutilation all over his body. Genitals hacked off. Deep gashes from knife wounds cut into his torso to slowly bleed him of life. And his eyelids had been sliced off, stakes driven into the ground on both sides of his head so that he was forced to stare into the sun. Flies buzzed and swarmed all over his blistered flesh. He was probably blind by now, and going mad, Jessie thought. It was a horrible way to die.

"I recognize him, one of the bounty hunters," Ki said, as they stood over the dying man.

"W-water . . . w-water . . ."

Jessie and Ki checked around them. A ring of jagged rock and boulders encircled the tabletop area, where this small plateau gave way to higher ground. The dying man kept pleading for water.

"Ki, do you want to go back to the horse and get a canteen? I mean, it's the least we can do. He's not going to last much longer."

Ki nodded and left to get the canteen. Jessie waited and sweated under the broiling sun. She sensed something around her, some invisible presence in the rocks above her, but she heard no sound. The buzzards circled lower, as if knowing a meal was only moments away from presenting itself to them.

Ki returned with the canteen. He uncapped it and knelt beside the bounty hunter.

"Who did this?" Ki asked the bounty hunter. "Was it Red Ghost?"

Then, just as Ki put the canteen to the man's lips, something whistled through the air. Ki jumped back as the arrow drilled through the bounty hunter's throat. The man cried out in pain, then gurgled on his own blood, which gushed from his mouth. He twitched in death throes then lay utterly still.

Jessie and Ki reached for their revolvers, but they didn't draw.

They didn't dare.

They rose over the rocks like demonic apparitions. There must've been fifty Apaches, Jessie decided, all of them with arrows drawn and pointed at them.

"Something tells me we're in a world of trouble, Jessie."

Jessie's heart pounded in her ears. She braced to shoot it out and go down fighting the second the first arrow was loosed. She looked up and behind them, only to find another dozen Apaches with arrows drawn. They were surrounded. It was eerie, she thought, how they had appeared out of nowhere, without the first sound. Tense, agonizing seconds passed, as Jessie thought for certain they were going to be drilled with enough arrows to make her and Ki look like pincushions.

Then a guttural shout sounded from somewhere above. It was a gruff male voice, talking in Apache. Slowly, every single Apache arrow was withdrawn from its bow. Jessie heaved a sigh of relief. She stood there beside Ki, sweating, waiting, her blood racing with adrenaline and an ice ball of fear lodged in her stomach.

Seconds later, the clopping of hooves sounded from somewhere behind Jessie and Ki. They turned to find an Apache astride a white stallion.

"Red Ghost," Ki breathed.

He was big for an Apache, Jessie decided, maybe six feet tall, judging by the way he sat, bareback, on his stallion. He had no headdress and no war paint, but he had a war club, a bow, a quiver stuffed with arrows, and a large hunting knife sheathed inside his belt. He had black hair that fell to his shoulders, which were broad and knotted with muscles. He was lean as a whip, and so muscular from the neck down it looked as if he had been carved out of stone. Two Apaches followed their chief on foot. Red Ghost stopped, ten feet short of Jessie and Ki. His dark eyes burned with anger and distrust as he sat there, staring at Jessie and Ki for several stretched seconds. He said something to his fellow warriors in his native tongue, and they answered him.

"You rode with bluebellies," Red Ghost said, his deep voice booming and rolling like thunder over the hill. It sounded like an accusation.

"We ride alone. We weren't with them," Jessie said.

"Woman who talks like she warrior," Red Ghost said. "Wears gun with look in her eyes like she can use it."

Jessie wasn't sure if he was saying that with contempt or admiration and amazement.

"You!" Red Ghost barked at Ki, then peered at him for a long moment. "You have not all white blood."

51

Ki swallowed hard. "I'm half-white."

Red Ghost seemed to think about something. Then a wry grin cut his lips, and he spoke to his warriors in Apache. The Apaches laughed.

"Half-white, only half-bad," Red Ghost said. He looked at Jessie, then said, "Give us white woman, you go free."

"No," Ki said. "We both go together or we don't go at all."

Red Ghost tensed, and fury darkened his face.

"You'll have to kill us both before I let that happen," Ki said. "That's my first and only offer, Chief."

Another long moment of angry quiet, then Red Ghost nodded, a strange smile on his lips. "You are brave. You would die for her?"

"Yes."

Red Ghost nodded. "I could kill you now and take her."

"I know that. But you'll have to kill us both. Neither one of us will go quietly to our deaths. You'll kill us, but you'll lose some warriors, too."

"You are strange man, Half-White Eyes." With catlike grace, Red Ghost leapt off his horse. He walked up to Jessie and Ki. Suddenly, he withdrew his knife.

Jessie and Ki draped their hands over their revolvers. In the blink of an eye, every single Apache had reloaded his bow and had it drawn.

Sunlight glinted off the razor-sharp steel of the blade in Red Ghost's hands. "Move away!"

Slowly, Jessie and Ki walked several steps away from the corpse. Red Ghost descended on the dead bounty hunter, and scalped him clean with one stroke of his blade. He stood there with his blood-dripping trophy in hand, his fierce stare going back and forth from Jessie to Ki.

"The men he was with, they ran from us like cowards last night," Red Ghost told them. "They kill my warriors when they have the power of numbers. They left their own behind to die. This white eyes deserved to die. Yes?"

Jessie decided to let Ki do the talking, not push her luck as the woman warrior. In Apache society, she knew, women were subordinate to men; they were to be seen and not heard.

"I think what you just said is true," Ki told the Apache chief. "They are bad men. The world would be a better place without them."

"White eyes soldiers, Captain Slaughter and his White Eyes Devils," Red Ghost said, "they will have to kill us, hunt us down. We will not go back to the reservation of your people."

"You're a free man. We have no quarrel with you," Ki told the Apache chief in a steady voice.

Red Ghost thrust his knife out to the side. "I go that way. Do not let our paths cross again. One of us would have to die if that happens. Your bravery has saved you. I look into your eyes. I see you are warrior."

Jessie saw the chief was pointing west with his knife. She was only too glad he wasn't pointing south, where they were heading.

"Go!" Red Ghost barked. "Cochillo Apono spares your life."

And Jessie and Ki left the plateau. Minutes later, they were mounted and riding south.

Ki let out a pent-up breath. "That was the

closest I think we've come to getting killed that I can remember, Jessie."

"You stood up to him, Ki. That was the only reason he let us go."

Ki cocked a wry grin. "Or maybe because I'm only a half-White Eyes?"

"Whatever. Let's just hope we don't run across Red Ghost again. Next time, we might not be so lucky to find him in such a generous mood."

To the west, Jessie saw the Apache war party riding on horseback, kicking up a wall of dust as they rode hard, away from the hills.

Jessie and Ki rode in silence for two hours. Other than the occasional tambourinelike noise of a rattler in the brush, or a scorpion crawling over rock, or a jackrabbit bounding in front of them, there was no sign of life. It was as if the burning plain had swallowed up any human life. Nothing but rock and cactus and jagged hills and a burning blue sky.

The sun was beginning to set beyond the sawtooth ridges of the hills to the west when Jessie and Ki came to the small town. There were maybe a half-dozen false-front structures, with perhaps twenty horses tethered to railings in front of the buildings. Several men with revolvers in holsters tied down to their thighs watched Jessie and Ki with suspicion and hostility as they rode into town. Jessie didn't recognize the gunmen.

Jessie and Ki dismounted in front of a building with a sign that read, Cantina. Pushing through the batwings, into the cantina, they found about fifteen gunmen sitting at round tables that were spread around the room. A big bearded man in a soiled white apron stood behind the bar, glaring at Jessie and Ki as they moved to the far corner of the room. There, Jessie and Ki took a table, keeping their backs to the wall. The silence in the cantina was broken only by the constant buzzing of flies.

"What are you drinking?" the bartender called out. "Got pulque, tequila, and beer."

Jessie gave the gunmen a quick eyeballing. They were all hard-eyed, grim-faced drifters caked in trail dust and drenched with sweat. Some of the gunmen played cards and swilled from whiskey bottles and smoked cigars, ignoring her altogether, while other gunmen stared at her with unconcealed lust. She didn't recognize any of these men either. There was a chance Judd Grimm had passed through this town, but nobody there looked all too eager to volunteer any information about the Grimm gang.

"How far is the Rio Grande?" Ki asked the bartender.

"Got about another ten-mile ride 'fore you hit the Mex border."

"What is this place?" Ki asked.

The bartender made a face as if Ki had asked a stupid question. "Just a town. A watering hole for drifters passing through here to Mexico."

"Got a name?"

"No."

Ki grunted. "How fitting. The town with no name. You got any law here?"

Jessie saw several gunmen tense at the question.

"Now, why the hell would you ask that? Dumb

damn question. Yeah, we got us a sheriff and a deputy, what damn good they do around here. I asked ya, what you drinkin'?"

"Water," Jessie said.

"Same here. What do you have to eat?"

"The usual and the only. Chili and bread. Want some?"

Jessie looked at Ki and shrugged. "Why not? I'm hungry."

"Bring it on," Ki told the bartender.

The bartender looked at Ki's bandaged head. "What happened to you?"

"I fell off my horse."

The bartender grunted something as he turned away. Moments later, he slapped two bowls of steaming chili down in front of Jessie and Ki, dug out spoons from his apron, and dropped them on the table.

Ki looked at the bartender. "Ask you a question?"

"Depends."

"Has a man by the name of Judd Grimm passed through here?"

Fear flickered through the barkeep's eyes. He hesitated long enough to tell Jessie he was going to lie.

"No, never heard the name," he said. "Get you that water. Suggest you eat and get the hell outta my place."

"What's the rush?" Jessie said. "Our money's good. We like your chili, we might want some more. We'd like that bread, too."

The barkeep grunted, spun on his heels, and went back to the bar.

Jessie felt the tension in the cantina thicken. She spooned some chili into her mouth. As the barkeep brought them their water and bread, Jessie noticed a gunman across the room stand and leave. She felt a freeze go down her spine. Something didn't feel right. The drifter, she sensed, had left with a sort of forced casualness. Ki watched the doorway, then looked at Jessie.

"You get the same bad feeling I get?" he asked Jessie in a low voice.

"Real bad."

Jessie looked beside them. There was a short hallway. At the end of the hallway there was a wooden door, which was closed. There was a plate-glass window beside the batwings at the front of the cantina, and Jessie kept her gaze fixed on the street. Her vigilance paid off. Seconds later, four shadows rolled over the window; then Judd Grimm burst through the batwings with his brother and two outlaws charging into the cantina behind him.

"I thought I got rid a you two!" Judd Grimm bellowed and began fanning the hammer of his revolver as Ki threw the table up into the air.

★

Chapter 6

Bullets peppered the table that Jessie and Ki used as a shield against the storm of lead. Revolvers in hand, they returned fire, braving the sizzling lead ripping off hunks of wood or ricocheting from the adobe wall behind them. A gunman standing beside Judd Grimm took a slug through the chest from Jessie's Colt and pitched through the batwings.

"Screw this! Gimme some sticks!" Judd Grimm bellowed.

Sticks! Ki knew what that meant. He saw that no other gunman in the room was making a move. They just sat, watching the ambush as if they were spectators to some game of faro. They'd be moving in a hurry in about two seconds, Ki knew.

"Come on, Jessie!" he yelled, grabbing her by the arm and rounding the corner to the hallway. As lead tracked them, and Ki saw several dynamite sticks sizzling and twirling through the air across the cantina, he dashed down the hallway. With every bit of strength he could command, fueled by fear and rage, he threw himself into the

58

door. There was an explosion of wood shards as Ki propelled himself through the doorway, then tumbled to the ground beyond the cantina. Behind him, Jessie nose-dived to the hard-packed soil as several tremendous explosions rocked the earth and fireballs were vomited out the back door. Chunks of debris and clouds of smoke blew over their heads. Then, seconds later, Ki's ears ringing with the blast, he stood beside Jessie. He saw the look of fierce determination in her eyes. They weren't about to let Grimm and his bunch leave town without a fight.

They ran around the side of the cantina, acrid clouds of smoke drifting over them. Horses without riders were whinnying and racing away from the ruins of the cantina. Then Jessie and Ki spotted Judd Grimm and his gang fleeing the carnage on horseback. They were heading south. Jessie and Ki began firing at the outlaws; then someone nearby roared, "Drop the guns! Now! You're under arrest!"

Jessie saw a tall, broad man with a star pinned to his chest aiming a Winchester rifle at them. A short, heavyset deputy with a revolver in hand ran beside the sheriff. They both closed on Jessie and Ki, and their weapons never wavered an inch off target.

"You know who those men are you're letting get away!?" Jessie growled.

"I don't give a damn who they are!" the sheriff said. "All I know is this here cantina just got blowed to bits, and you're the reason for hell coming to town. I'll cover them, Deputy. You take their weapons. Either one of you so much as blinks I'll plug you where you stand."

Jessie looked at the smoke billowing out of the gaping maw in front of the cantina. It didn't look as if anyone had survived the blasts. Even their mounts had been killed during the explosions, their torn and twisted carcasses outstretched in the rubble. Jessie cursed this sudden misfortune. They were innocent, and now they were going to jail in a no-name town in the middle of nowhere. She was afraid the only justice for them would be the hanging kind.

"We were just defending our lives. They came in, blasting away!" Ki said. "Those men who just left your town, Sheriff, they're outlaws who have killed about two dozen people in the past couple of days."

"That a fact? Well, if I can find any witnesses in the ashes who can verify that, you can be on your way," the sheriff said.

The deputy stripped Jessie and Ki of their weapons.

More than an hour had passed since Jessie and Ki had been thrown in the same cell together. Neither the sheriff nor the deputy had come back to the jail office after locking them up. But through the iron-barred window in front of the office Ki could see the lawmen sifting in the rubble.

"Do you think a jailbreak is out of the question?" he said, a grim smile on his lips.

The sheriff and the deputy returned.

"I'm Sheriff Rupert Barnes and this is Deputy Markin. No one except for you two lived through those blasts. Kinda funny, don't you think, that you were the only two to escape?"

"How many times do we have to tell you, Sheriff, it wasn't us who threw the dynamite," Jessie said. "And we weren't the only ones who escaped without a scratch."

"Well, you two are just gonna have to sit, until I figure out what to do with you."

"Why don't you go after the men who leveled the cantina?" Jessie said.

"I intend to do just that, missie," the sheriff said. "Soon as I can get some marshals down here."

"They'll be across the border by then, Sheriff, probably disappear into San Pedro," Jessie said. "You have heard of San Pedro, haven't you, Sheriff? It's a haven for outlaws. Probably a lot of those outlaws pass through your town with no name."

"That supposed to be some kinda accusation, missie?"

"Take it however you want to, Sheriff. What I'm saying is you let us go, well, we were after those men. We can get them."

"You two?" the deputy said, smirking. "All by yourselves, you're going to go hunt them down."

Jessie and Ki said nothing. Further talk seemed pointless and hopeless. There seemed no way out.

Then fate smiled on them.

Ki heard the clopping of dozens of hooves beyond the jail office. Then he saw the uniforms.

"What the hell's this?" the sheriff gruffed. "Why's the cavalry come to town?"

Jessie and Ki moved to the front of the jail cell and grasped the bars as Captain Frederick rolled

61

through the doorway and introduced himself to the sheriff.

"I heard what happened, and I want these people released immediately," the Captain announced, "to my custody."

"Says who?" the sheriff growled.

The Captain flung some official-looking papers into the sheriff's lap. "The United States Government. If you read those carefully, you'll see I have full power of command over any jurisdiction in Texas, and I have the right to usurp any authority, as ordered by the governor of this state. And we are still in Texas, Sheriff. If you'd be so kind."

"Damn." The sheriff flung the papers back at the Captain. "Let 'em go. Damn it, Captain, they just ride into my town, blow up a cantina, I got bits and pieces of maybe twenty men to pick up, and you waltz right in here and want them to go scot-free."

"Did you listen to their side of their story? Such as, they were attacked first perhaps. They don't carry dynamite, if you'd checked their saddlebags."

Scowling, the deputy opened the door to the cell.

After retrieving their weapons, Jessie and Ki walked up to the Captain as he stood in the doorway.

"Thank you, Captain," Jessie said. "No telling how long we would have sat in there. Does this mean we ride with you again?"

"That's exactly right. Let's get out of here."

Outside, Jessie saw that the ranks of soldiers had been seriously cut down during the death march. Jessie saw there were extra horses with saddles among the troops.

"Captain, our horses were killed during the blast."

"Take your pick. I have plenty of extra mounts now."

She thanked him. Then Jessie and Ki went and got their saddlebags, picked out two geldings, and mounted. They rode up to the Captain, who was now in the saddle at the head of the line.

"I have forty-five men left," the Captain said, scowling. "I still don't know who attacked us in the gorge. It was either the bounty hunters or the Grimm gang. Whoever it was, they'll pay when we catch up to them. Morale is bad and my men are on edge. They have very itchy trigger fingers right now. And you're right, if I hadn't happened along, you'd still be sitting in there. It just so happened we spent the better part of yesterday and today looking for Apaches in the mountains north of here, or we would've already been across the border. Unfortunately, Red Ghost is living up to his reputation. It's as if he can vanish into thin air."

Knowing it wouldn't help the Captain's situation or the morale of the troops, neither Jessie nor Ki mentioned their encounter with Red Ghost.

"When we finally do hit San Pedro, if this General Alfredo doesn't hand over the men on my list, then he's going to have a bloody fight on his hands," the Captain said.

"General Alfredo," Jessie murmured to herself, wondering all of a sudden why that name was trying to ring a bell.

"What's the matter, Jessie?" Ki asked.

Jessie dug out the black book from her saddlebag. In the book were the names of men in the cabal who had murdered her father. And Jessie found General Paco Alfredo's name in the book.

"He's in the book, Ki," Jessie said. "I knew that name sounded familiar."

"What book?" the Captain asked.

Jessie explained briefly about her father, his murder, and the book he had left behind implicating the men in the cabal.

"So, you're going to take out the good general also?" the Captain said. "Sounds like you're a lady with a lot of scores to settle. Well, I tell you what, I have a plan. When we break for camp for the night near the border, I'll tell it to you."

Jessie nodded as the column headed out. She'd hear out the Captain's plan. If she didn't like it, she'd come up with a plan of her own.

At nightfall, they crossed the shallow, muddy waters of the Rio Grande and found an abandoned village a mile inside the Mexican border. There were maybe thirty adobe huts nestled at the base of a chain of hills. The Captain ordered his men to set up camp in the ghost town for the night, secure the perimeter. Soldiers broke out kerosene lanterns and lit them. In the soft sheen of lamplight, Jessie could see bullet holes and other much bigger jagged holes, from cannon fire, in several of the huts. The town had probably come under siege during the Mexican War.

Jessie and Ki dismounted beside the Captain in front of a hut at the end of the street. This hut appeared undamaged by whatever past battle had raged here.

"I'm going to make my quarters here," the Captain announced. "I have a good bottle of brandy. Would you care for some, Miss Jessie? We can discuss my plan inside."

Ki must have seen this as some cue to make himself scarce. If he was offended over not being invited inside with the Captain and Jessie, he didn't show it. Instead, he nodded and said, "I need to rest. Jessie, you can fill me in later. Dismissed, Captain?" Ki said, but smiled.

The Captain returned Ki's smile. "You're a good man, Ki. I wish I had a hundred like you under my command."

Ki didn't acknowledge the compliment. As he departed to join the soldiers securing the town, Jessie followed the Captain inside the adobe hut. A soldier had already lit a lantern and placed it on a table for the Captain. The Captain put the bottle of brandy down on the table and dismissed the soldier, after telling him he didn't want to be disturbed unless they were attacked, and that no one was to be posted at his door.

Jessie checked out their surroundings. Aside from the table and several wooden chairs, there was some clay pottery strewn around the room and some blankets piled in a far corner. She looked at the Captain as he beckoned her to sit down. She sensed there was more to this meeting than the Captain wanting to discuss some plan of action against General Alfredo. She was intrigued by this man, and she couldn't deny she felt a strong attraction for the Captain. She sat, accepted his glass of brandy, and sipped it. This night, she thought, could prove very interesting.

The Captain sipped at his own glass. He looked Jessie dead in the eye. "I ask myself, why would such a beautiful woman want to be out here, hunting outlaws and killers? And the answer I come up with is that there's more to you than just beauty. You've got a lot of heart, a lot of class, and a lot of guts. I don't think I've ever met a woman like you anywhere."

"Are you saying you've been trying to control yourself, Captain, in order to keep morale up?"

He chuckled. "That's a good way of putting it. Maybe I'm just being plain selfish at the moment, thinking about my own morale. I've always loved beautiful women. I could never settle down with just one woman, not on any permanent basis. Which is why I suppose I may die single."

"Well, then, I have a confession to make also."

"Oh? What?"

Jessie sipped her brandy, drawing out the silence. There was a presence, a strong force, about this man she found herself becoming less and less able to resist. She wanted him; it was that simple.

"I've been wondering when there might come a time when I could test troop morale."

The Captain looked long and hard at Jessie. Then a warm smile creased his lips. He looked toward the corner of the room, at the blankets. "How about now?"

"Why not?"

The Captain turned the lantern down low, then led Jessie to the far corner of the room. There, in the deep shadows, he shook the blankets out. Jessie looked him deep in the eye and saw his desire for her burning in his stare. She felt her blood race with her own hunger and anticipation. Gently, he placed his hands on her face, drew her to him, and kissed her. He kissed her softly, probing her mouth with his tongue. Then he began kissing her neck with smooth, soft pecks, his hands sliding down to her buttocks, where he began squeezing and kneading her cheeks. She let herself go limp, wanting the total force of this man to consume her. She found the situation intriguing, and exciting because of the risk of getting caught in the act by a wandering soldier. She was with the man who had total authority over dozens of lives, and she was going to be with him. He was a good man, a strong man, and she'd always had a soft spot in her heart for such men.

She felt his strength rise as he brushed his manhood against her. Quickly, after checking the doorway and finding no roving soldiers, they undressed and slid beneath the blankets. She took his swollen, throbbing member in her hand and began stroking it as their mouths locked in long, hot kisses. He was big and it was hot to the touch, and she found herself moistening quickly, her legs parting, eager to accept him into her. He rubbed her breasts, playing with her nipples; then he sucked her breasts, while sticking a finger into her slippery juices.

Jessie squirmed and moaned with pleasure. A cool night breeze drifted through the room, but sweat was rolling down her back as she writhed with his light teasing of her wetness. He stroked the length of her long, creamy legs, then kneaded her taut, round buttocks some more. He rolled on top of her and slowly eased himself into her. Jessie let out a soft cry as he speared her deep. She drew her legs back as he began driving in and out. She dug her fingers into the hard muscles of his shoulders, pulling him to her as she fought to achieve orgasm. She almost exploded, but he pulled out and rolled her over. She felt him spreading her cheeks wide, as he entered her from behind, thrusting deep into her fiery juices. He cupped a breast, squeezing it, rolling the nipple around in his finger. This was some of the most impulsive and spontaneous sex Jessie had had in a long time, and she found herself becoming dizzy with excitement and with the fear in the back of her mind that some soldier was going to walk in on them or that Red Ghost and his Apaches might attack any second. But all she wanted right then was this moment and this man. The world, the death hunt, would have to wait.

She felt his hot lips on her neck, his hands prying her ass apart as he slowed his motion, teasing her as he gently withdrew himself, then eased his member into her again. She bucked against him, slapping her cheeks into him as she strained at the brink of exploding. It was as if he wouldn't let her erupt with pleasure; he wanted it to last, pulling out just as she was about to reach orgasm. Finally, he rolled her over on her back again. She pulled her legs back as far as they would go as he slid into her, splitting her again with his massive length and girth. She burned inside, thought her whole body would explode from passion. Finally, she did explode, and she lay there, quivering and convulsing with orgasm, her lips locked on his mouth as wave after wave of pleasure tore through her.

And he still wasn't finished with her.

He rolled beneath her, keeping her impaled on him. She rode him with a frenzy, her blond mane cool and damp against her bare shoulders, from free-flowing sweat. She gnashed her teeth, rubbing herself against him with a feeling of desperation and passion that was still flaming. He was still as hard as a rock, as she slid, up and down, on his rigid pole. She was going crazy with desire. Then she exploded with yet another orgasm. She shook her head, her hair whipping around her face as she groaned and clawed his chest, his hands filled with her big, firm breasts. She couldn't take it anymore; she had to feel him release himself in her, and she told him to do just that. She squeezed his sac as he spread her cheeks wide. Then he kissed her, and after several deep upward thrusts, she felt him erupt a stream of hot juices into her. For several minutes they lay there in each other's arms and sweat.

"You are some kind of woman, Jessie Starbuck."

"And you, Captain, you're some kind of man. But I think we'd better get dressed. Troop morale, remember. I wouldn't want them to see you caught with your pants down with the only woman for miles around."

"Right. We came in here to discuss the plan."

They dressed and moved back to the table. The Captain took a sip of brandy, then went to the door to check on his troops. Apparently, there was nothing out of the ordinary, so he returned to the table.

"All's well with the troops?" Jessie asked, smiling as she sipped her brandy.

"For the moment. Now, uh, where were we?"

"We were having fun. Now it's back to business. Maybe just for the moment?"

The Captain looked a little embarrassed. "I took a chance."

"You mean you're having regrets?"

"None at all. But we can't do that again. That's why I wanted that moment to last."

"It did. It was a long moment."

The Captain cleared his throat, sat silent for a moment, then said, "Okay, here's what I have in mind. I don't intend to just ride right into San Pedro and demand this General Alfredo and his federales hand over the men I have on my list. What I would like for you and Ki to do is to ride in, just like you're passing through. A simple recon. Scout the situation, get a feel for the numbers. We'll ride within seeing distance of the town; we'll watch and wait as you and Ki go into San Pedro. If trouble breaks out . . . well, then we'll have no choice but to ride in and take matters into our own hands."

"And if the Grimm gang or the bounty hunters are there?"

"Is it a risk you're willing to take?"

Jessie thought long and hard about that. It seemed like a logical course of action, but she had no idea what they would be walking into in San Pedro. If the Grimm gang or the bounty hunters were there, then all hell would break loose in a heartbeat. But she had a mission, just as the Captain did. And where there was no risk, there was no gain.

"I'll talk it over with Ki, but I don't think he'll have any problem with your plan."

"Good." He paused. "Then I guess this will have to be good night. If you were to sleep here, well, you want to talk about all hell breaking loose."

Jessie chuckled, finished her brandy. Smiling, cherishing the moment she had just shared with him, she looked deep into the Captain's eyes. "Good night."

Outside, she found Ki halfway down the street. He was sitting in front of a hut, sipping from his canteen. He looked up at Jessie and smiled.

"By the looks of that twinkle in your eye, I gather the meeting went well?" Ki said.

"I think love and war sometimes go hand in hand."

Ki grunted. "So, aside from the love, what's going on with the Captain's war?"

"He wants us to do some scouting for him."

★

Chapter 7

It was just before the first light of dawn broke across the sky when they moved out of the abandoned Mexican village.

As usual, Jessie and Ki rode up front with the Captain. If the troops suspected a liaison had occurred between her and their commanding officer, she didn't see any hint of it in their eyes. No resentment. No leers. No whispered conversations. Instead, she overheard talk from several soldiers who had lost loved ones to the renegade Apaches, about how they wanted some Indian scalps to take back to Fort Mason. The mood was ugly, thick with anger and frustration. Captain Frederick was right—these soldiers were on edge. Gut instinct warned her there would be trouble in San Pedro. For starters, the federales would be insulted that the U.S. Army had ridden down into their country to demand the extradition, or in this instance perhaps the execution, of wanted outlaws and renegade Indians. For finishers, these soldiers were not about to go back across the Rio Grande empty-handed.

They encountered no one out there on the sweeping desert floor. It was close to noon when a range of hills loomed to the south under the fiery orange eye of the sun. This time the Captain didn't send any scouts ahead. Sergeant Milrose informed him that San Pedro was just beyond the hills, according to his map.

They found a gorge that cut through the hills, then came across a gully which they climbed to the top, and Jessie and Ki found themselves staring down at San Pedro, about two miles south. It was a sprawling place, crowded with rows of adobe buildings, and it looked to be teeming with people. From the largest building to the east, the Mexican flag hung from a pole. That would be General Alfredo's quarters, Jessie suspected, the palace of San Pedro. She was eager to pay the General a personal visit. Exactly how he had been involved with the cabal that had killed her father, she wasn't sure. It didn't matter. General Paco Alfredo was a target.

The Captain ordered the area to be secured, then told Jessie and Ki, "A quick but thorough reconnaissance. Then come back. If you're not back in two hours, I will assume there's been trouble. If that happens, we'll come down for you. Good luck."

Jessie nodded, then urged her mount back down the gully.

"There's going to be a war, you know that, don't you, Jessie? Those soldiers are primed to kill."

Jessie said nothing, but she couldn't have agreed more with what Ki had just said.

• • •

Jessie and Ki were met with suspicion and hostility when they rode into San Pedro. Maybe a half dozen narrow dirt streets cut the rows of adobe dwellings as they forged deeper into the city. Laughter and shouting sounded from cantinas. Mules and horses, chickens and dogs wandered aimlessly through the streets. Half-naked urchins laughed and pointed at the two of them. It was the men, though, who sent a chill down Jessie's spine. There were dozens of hard-looking men, all of them with revolvers in tied-down holsters. She found Mexicans, Indians, and white men roaming the streets, but she only found a few Mexicans in the uniform of the federales. Dark-skinned, dark-haired women were fondled in doorways by gunmen, but they managed to stop the groping long enough to cast Jessie a wary and jealous eye. Whistles and calls of *"Gringita!"* hit Jessie's backside.

"I think the Captain's going to need more than a few dozen men to handle this town," Ki commented, as they kept slowly riding down the widest street. Jessie kept the General's palace in sight in the distance, perched on a short rise. If Judd Grimm or the bounty hunters were there in San Pedro, they would be hard, if not impossible, to find.

"Hombre, how much for blondie!?"

Jessie reined her mount in as a group of five Mexican men blocked their path. They were drunk, swilling almost constantly from bottles of pulque as they leered at Jessie, staggered around, and nudged each other in the ribs. Trouble.

74

"I'm afraid you've badly mistaken my friend here for a whore," Ki said in an icy voice. "Step aside."

Their faces darkened with fury. Jessie knew what was coming next. But as soon as they reached for their revolvers both she and Ki had their own weapons out, hammers cocked. A hard silence seemed instantly to descend over the street, and all activity stopped. The five Mexicans kept their hands draped over the butts of their revolvers. Jessie felt dozens of eyes boring into her. Killing was probably commonplace here; in fact, she thought, it was most likely an interesting way to pass time in San Pedro.

"Don't," Ki warned. "You'll be very sorry, amigos."

They didn't listen.

"*Hijo de la chingada!*" one of the Mexican gunmen roared, then drew his revolver, the other four *bandidos* following his lead.

Jessie and Ki opened up, their revolvers flaming and bucking and spitting out a lightning lead storm. Their deadly accurate fire swept the line of *bandidos*, pinching them in a scissoring march of lead. Blood spurted from their soiled white shirts as they spun and toppled and fired off wild rounds at the sky. Jessie and Ki held on tight to the reins of their mounts as their horses whinnied and danced. One gunman hit his knees, clutching his chest, but as he aimed at Jessie, both Jessie and Ki pumped rounds into him, slamming him to the ground. Dust settled over the dead, and flies swarmed over their twitching, bloody meat.

"Drop your weapons! Now!"

Jessie and Ki turned to find a half dozen federales running toward them, aiming flintlock carbines with fixed bayonets. Jessie and Ki looked at each other with resignation. They had no choice. Again. They dropped their weapons.

"I think a few words with the General can settle this matter," Jessie told the federales.

"*Silencio! Puta!*"

They were marched by the federales into a banquet hall at the palace. There were meats and cheese and bread and fruit spread down a long, wide table, but very little eating was going on. Uniformed Mexicans and American *pistoleros* lounged around the hall, drinking and smoking, or groping and grappling with dark-skinned, scantily clad whores. Abrupt silence fell over the hall as Jessie and Ki were led to General Alfredo.

He sat at the head of the table, a whore in his lap, a bottle of pulque in his free hand. He was dressed in the heavily embroidered uniform of a division general, and he was also clearly drunk. He stood, shoving the whore away, a scowl on his swarthy face as he took several lurching steps away from the table. Jessie was surprised at how short the General was; she figured he stood no more than five and a half feet tall. He had a sword in an ornately carved sheath and a flintlock pistol tucked inside his waistband. Despite being short, Jessie sensed the General was a man who could intimidate others with just a flash of his dark, burning eyes. A federale piled Jessie and Ki's weapons at the General's feet, while another

76

soldier whispered something in his ear. He waved the soldier away, took a deep swig from his bottle, then nodded several times, raking Jessie and Ki over with a cold stare.

"A man whose heritage I cannot determine," the General said, "and a blond *gringita*, ride into my town and kill five men like expert gunfighters, as easy as I might step on a scorpion. But . . . I know why you are here. *Sí*, General Paco Alfredo, he knows everything that happens in his city. I am like, should we say, God." He laughed. "I see all, I hear all, I know all. And I have the power of life and death."

Jessie felt an ice ball lodge in her guts. Knows why we're here? she thought. And Ki tensed, glancing at Jessie, as a side door behind the table opened.

And Judd Grimm and his gang walked out into the banquet hall. They stood behind the General like conquering heroes. There were now only eight outlaws of the Grimm gang left. Jessie recalled that she had dropped Priestley over the gold cache, and Ki had drilled an outlaw just before being blown off the hill.

"Hello, folks," Judd Grimm said, smiling. "I kinda been expecting you. Looks like we beat you here. Damn, but you two have a lotta luck on your side. 'Fraid, though, your luck's maybe run out."

"Are you not going to say hello to my good ami-go, Judd Grimm?" the General said, and laughed.

"Be surprised what a little bit of gold can do for a man down here," Judd Grimm told Jessie and Ki.

"Thees, his brother, Eli," the General said, pointing at a skinny, ferret-faced gunman standing beside his brother. "Thees, Robert Feller. Forgive me, hombres, I do not know the rest of your names."

"Don't matter, General," a short, stocky outlaw with chipped teeth said. "Long as you keep us outta harm's way."

"And as long as I get my payment of gold every month," the General said, and laughed.

Suddenly, the big double doors to the banquet hall burst open. A federale raced up beside the General and said something to him in Spanish.

"It would seem we have company," the General said, glowering at Jessie and Ki. "*Soldados*. Leave. Lieutenant Alvarez will take you," he told Judd Grimm. "You will not come out until I tell you to."

"Soldiers," one of the outlaws said. "Shit. They came down here for us, General."

"They ain't gonna leave without us, General," Eli Grimm said. "They'll tear this town apart to find us."

"Maybe they do not come for you!" the General barked. "Move!"

Cursing, the outlaws left the banquet hall through the same door by which they had entered.

Jessie and Ki looked at each other, tense and worried. Moments later, Jessie saw Captain Frederick, Sergeant Milrose, and twelve other soldiers striding into the banquet hall.

"What is meaning of this?" General Alfredo boomed. "*Yanqui* soldiers in Mexico. I was not aware we were at war with your country again."

Captain Frederick walked right up to the General and introduced himself. "There will be a war, General, but only if you don't cooperate."

The General's gaze narrowed as something dangerous flashed through his eyes. "One squad of soldiers, *Capitán*, and you think you can take on me and my federales. We number sixty in San Pedro. And there are many men who lost brothers in the war between our countries. They would be most eager to spill your blood."

"Well, I have about forty more soldiers outside, General. The odds would be on your side, but you'd lose a lot of men. Believe me. Now. Please. We are not here to start a war."

"Then what do you want? Why are you here?"

"I have a list here of outlaws, Americans, who are believed to have crossed the border and to be hiding in your town. I want to find them. I'll weed them out, hunt them down, whatever I have to do. But they are wanted by my government, and I have been granted permission to do whatever is necessary to bring them back to justice."

The General scowled. "You burst in here, make demands, in short, you insult me here with your presence and insinuations that I may be harboring criminals. I am truly shocked!"

Jessie chuckled at that. Ki shook his head.

"*Silencio!* Say nothing, or you will all die!" the General roared at Jessie and Ki.

Jessie could see that the General was insane. He was at the point of erupting into mindless violence.

79

"These people, General, they are my friends," the Captain said. "I want them turned over to my custody."

"Your amigos? In that case, I must say no. You see, *Capitán*, they ride into San Pedro and spill Mexican blood. What justice is there for the men they killed? I cannot let them just walk. It would make me look very bad."

"Then let the woman go," Ki said. "I'll stay. You can do what you wish with me."

The General looked at Ki, long and hard, then chuckled. He sipped some more pulque. "No. I have a better idea. This is my offer to you, *Capitán*. You will like it, or you and your men and these two, none of you will leave here alive."

The General draped his fist over his flintlock pistol. Federales aimed their rifles at Captain Frederick and his soldiers.

Jessie tensed, prepared to make a dash for her weapons, sensing that violence was about to erupt.

"Are you ready to hear my offer, *Capitán?*"

Jessie saw Captain Frederick fist the butt of his revolver, his face cold with anger. All hell was about to break loose.

★

Chapter 8

The General waited for Captain Frederick's reply.

Jessie felt her blood race like wildfire, certain gunplay was about to explode. Jessie and Ki would be caught in the cross fire between the warring soldiers.

"*Capitán!?* I am waiting!"

A hard pause, then Captain Frederick said, "Let's hear it."

The General smiled, nodded. "*Bueno.*"

"Get those goddamn rifles pointed away from me and my men."

The General snapped his fingers, and his men lowered their rifles. "Now. We can talk like reasonable men. Thees is what I offer. You and your soldiers, you have free movement in my city, you can hunt whoever these men are, you can even keel them if you have to, or if you want to." Again, he laughed. "But . . . you have until nightfall. And . . . if you kill anyone other than a gringo, you will answer to me."

The Captain looked confused. "That's it?"

"No. That is not it. As, eh, shall we say, for

insurance, I will keep the *gringita* here with me. To make sure, you understand, that you comply with my instructions."

Jessie saw Ki take a step toward the General, his eyes burning with rage. She dropped a hand over his shoulder and stopped him from charging the General.

The General became incensed. "You have problem with that, hombre?"

"Yes, I do," Ki said.

"Ki, I'll be fine. I'll handle the situation," Jessie told her bodyguard.

The General leered at Jessie. "*Sí*, you will handle the situation. You will be my guest. You will eat, drink. We will talk and become friends, no?"

"Probably, no," Jessie said, "but I don't see where I have any choice."

The General's face hardened. "That is right. You do not have a choice."

Captain Frederick muttered a curse. "All right, General, we'll do it your way. Nightfall. By then, you turn that woman over to me. No matter what. If you do not . . . believe me, there will be a war. And I suggest to you that you see no harm comes to her. Ki, let's go."

Reluctantly, Ki gave Jessie one last look. She told him to go, that she'd be fine.

"Take your weapons, hombre," the General told Ki. "A man can never be too careful in San Pedro. A man without a weapon here is, how shall I say, eh, like a man without *cajones*," he said and laughed. "I would not want you to lose your pride and joy."

Outlaws and whores laughed at Ki.

He retrieved his weapons, then moved and stood beside Captain Frederick.

"Hombre," the General said to Ki. "So you know they are here." He shrugged and laughed. "I know you will tell the good Captain. Good luck in finding them. If you do, maybe you find the rest of their gold, eh? Maybe we work something out?"

"What the Captain told you about the woman, that goes double for me," Ki said.

Jessie watched as Ki, the Captain, and his soldiers left the banquet hall. She felt the General's laughing gaze boring into the back of her head. She turned and saw the General motioning for her to sit at the head of the table with him. She frowned, looking around the big room at the dozens of gunmen and whores watching her. She moved and sat beside the General, who shoveled a slab of meat into his mouth.

"Eat! It will do you good."

Jessie decided that the best way to kill time until nightfall might be to eat a little something, even indulge the General. But only in conversation. If he tried anything else, she'd have his flintlock in her hand and shoved down his gullet in an eye blink.

She intended to do just that anyway. But she decided to wait until the General was just a little more drunk.

"Guamo!"

Jessie followed the General's stare across the room. In the far corner of the hall she saw, stepping away from a group of gunmen, a mountain of a man with shoulder-length black hair. Guamo.

He had a huge hunting knife inside a black leather sash, and he was so muscular he appeared to be carved out of granite. He was barefoot and wore only baggy white cotton pants.

"Guamo," the General told Jessie, his mouth full of food. "He is Yaqui. Very big for Indian, no? He is also very skilled with that knife of his. He will keep an eye on your friend for me. Guamo, step up, I have work for you."

Work? Jessie thought. She didn't like the sound of that. But Ki, she knew, could take care of himself. If the General was looking to start a war, then a war, she thought, was what he would get.

And a war was what Jessie most certainly anticipated happening in San Pedro before the day was over.

Ki was furious at having to leave Jessie behind under the General's leering eye. If anything happened to Jessie between now and nightfall, he would kill any and everything that moved in the palace. Then again, he decided, he just might go back there on his own, open fire, and take his chances anyway.

Outside, Ki and Captain Frederick and his soldiers mounted their horses.

"You actually believe that the General is going to let you pick his town apart and shoot it out with any outlaws we find?" Ki said to the Captain.

"Don't be so cynical, Ki. I'm here to do a job, and I'll move heaven, hell, and earth to do it. Sergeant! Break out those wanted posters. Let's get to work. We've only got to sundown."

"And then what, Captain?" Ki queried, easing his mount ahead, beside Captain Frederick, as the cavalry moved down the widest dirt street, dozens of villagers watching them with hostility and suspicion.

"Then, Ki, my good friend, we go back to the palace and take Jessie with us. Even if we have to shoot it out with the federales. Until then, I'll have to take the General at his word."

Ki decided to tell Captain Frederick the score. "You want to hear about the General's word, Captain? He's hiding Judd Grimm and his bunch. They paid him gold. They left the banquet hall just before you entered."

The Captain snorted. "Well, I would've expected as much. Any way it's cut, Ki, we're on our own. We'll get Grimm and his gang, too. I'm not about to leave here with a handful of nothing."

They moved off an intersecting street. The sweltering air was rife with the stench of urine and feces and vomit. Everywhere Ki heard the sounds of drunken laughter, or vomiting, or cursing, noises which drowned out the clop of dozens of hooves from the cavalry. Clouds of flies buzzed around Ki's face and the faces of the soldiers. The damnable flies were inescapable; they were like some curse of nature, he thought. Several Mexican men in sombreros openly cursed the soldiers. This was the meanest, ugliest town Ki had ever set foot in.

"Hey, Cap'n!"

Ki swiveled his head to find a stoop-shouldered man as old as time and with a toothless mouth grinning at the Captain. He had a long, flowing white beard and deep-set rheumy eyes.

"Name's Zachariah Ornsby."

"So, what can I do for you?"

"Listen, heh-heh, word is yer lookin' for *pistoleros* from across the border. Maybe I can help. Maybe they's somethin' in it for me?"

"Make your pitch. I don't have all day."

The old man cackled. Ki thought he was insane.

"Well, been down here now nary five years, maybe six. Seen lots a bad men come and go through San Pee-dro. You lookin' for *pistoleros*, that true?"

"If you can help me, you can help me; if you can't, then step aside."

"Now, now, Cap'n, that ain't no way to treat a fellow American. Sheeit. Got some paper on ya, lemme take a look-see."

"Sergeant!"

Ki watched as Sergeant Milrose handed the old man a batch of wanted posters. The old man took his time. He nodded, scratching his beard. He grunted, spat, rifled through the papers, then farted and said " 'Scuse me, Cap'n. Chili down here's a real killer on the ol' plumbing."

"I'm losing patience, mister."

"Now, now. I got what you want. See them here," the old man said, showing the Captain several of the posters. "That's Will Feeney and Bart Milligan, and looks like you got about eight more in there of his gang. Came down two weeks ago."

"Are they still here?"

The old man fingered his beard. "Eh . . . could be, yup, just could be."

"I asked you a question, mister! This is official United States Army business. If you know something, it would be in your best interest to tell it to me."

"What I need to know first, Cap'n . . . Well, I wanna know what kinda deal we can strike up."

"Deal?"

"Yup. You git 'em, I want whatever they's got in their pockets and in their saddlebags."

"Why, you old buzzard!" Sergeant Milrose snarled.

The old man cackled. "Yup, sonny, that's me. Ol' Buzzard. How'd you know that was my nickname? Heh-heh."

"All right, old-timer," the Captain said. "In other words, you'll lead us to them, but only if I let you have your way with their belongings."

"Now you got me."

The Captain scowled, his beard soaked with sweat as he sat on his mount, broiling under the sun, a cloud of flies swarming about him. "It's a deal."

The old man cackled, walked out in front of the Captain's mount, and pointed toward a cantina at the end of the street. "Saw 'em go in there, 'bout an hour ago. They mean and crazy, I warn ya. They see ya, no tellin', they just might start shootin'. Heard 'em braggin' ain't no law ever goin' take them back alive. Be right here, Cap'n. 'Spect there'll be some trouble, so you don't mind, I'll just stan' here an' watch. Hope you're a man of your word."

"And I hope you're not giving me a bum lead, mister."

The old man shook his head. "Nope. Not when I know they got about three grand in American dollars in their pockets. I may be old and crazy, but I ain't stupid. Good luck, Cap'n."

They moved out toward the cantina. Ki looked behind him. Just then, at the opposite end of the street, he spotted a huge man dressed only in white cotton pants, with a large hunting knife inside a sash. Even through the thin sheet of dust trailing the cavalry he would've sworn the stranger was staring him right in the eye. Villagers moved away from the stranger, seemed to regard him with fear. Who was he? Ki wondered. A killer sent by General Alfredo to keep an eye on the gringos? If he ran into him, or even saw him again, Ki intended to find out who he was and what he wanted. He had too many problems to deal with to have some stranger dogging his every move.

The cantina where the suspected fugitives were hiding was a long, low-lying adobe building. Outside there was a railing with maybe twenty horses hitched to it. The Captain signaled with his hand, and his men moved out to form a long line in front of the cantina. They looked like a firing squad, and Ki suspected that's exactly what they were meant to be. Ki sat beside the Captain, staring at the open doorway. They sat in silence, waiting. Excited jabber hit Ki's back as villagers gathered around in the street.

Finally, three, then four, then five white *pistoleros* lurched through the doorway. They were drunk. It took them several stretched seconds to realize they had their backs pressed to the wall by almost fifty American soldiers. Three more gunmen then staggered out into the street.

"Feeney, Milligan, I'm Captain Frederick of the United States Army. You and your men are under arrest."

"The hell we are! You ain't takin' us alive, asshole!"

The old man was right, Ki saw: The outlaws were not going back alive. All eight of them drew their revolvers, almost at the same instant. They were prepared to commit suicide rather than go back to face justice in the United States.

They died were they stood.

Several outlaws fired off shots, and two soldiers spilled from their mounts with ragged crimson holes in their chests. Then dozens of soldiers began blazing away with revolvers and repeater rifles. The outlaws screamed and cursed as they were scythed apart by the hellish barrage of lead. They danced and spun, bloody sieves that were pinned to the adobe wall of the cantina, which was sprayed with great arcs and smears of blood. Horses whinnied and snapped their reins free of the railing, racing off down the street. Dust and clouds of cordite hung over the soldiers as they kept pumping lead into the outlaws, crucifying them against the blood-drenched adobe wall. It was more than enough. Ki had his Remington out, but he didn't fire off a shot, simply because he didn't need to. The Captain and his soldiers had taken care of any danger by slaughtering the outlaws in a few seconds.

But the danger wasn't over.

A woman was screaming hysterically as an outlaw bulled through the cantina doorway, his arm locked around her throat, a gun pressed to her head.

"Don't do it, or this Mex bitch dies!" the outlaw roared.

"Hold your fire!" the Captain bellowed at his troops.

A second later, another outlaw appeared. This outlaw had a small boy as a hostage, and he had a gun pressed to the boy's head. Both men looked every bit as desperate as the others, their eyes filled with the same suicidal rage that Ki had seen in their dead comrades' eyes.

Ki slid off his mount. He pulled a *shuriken* from his vest, and, crouching, he moved down the rear of the line of soldiers, keeping the outlaws and their hostages in grim death sights.

"That's right, Cap'n, just be a good little soldier boy and I'll just get the hell outta here and nobody else has to die!"

"I'll kill this brat, too, you so much as point a gun at me!"

Ki hit the end of the line of soldiers. It was a daring move, perhaps crazy, but there was no choice. He hurled the *shuriken*, and the twirling throwing star speared into the exposed leg of the outlaw with the woman hostage. As the woman broke free, screaming and running down the street, Ki shot the outlaw with the boy in the forehead, then swung his Remington and drew a bead on the outlaw with the throwing star in his leg. Ki didn't have to fire the first round, because a loud volley of shots rang out and tore the outlaw apart, his head exploding, his chest and stomach erupting under the terrible rain of bullets.

Long moments of tight silence hung over the street as the last outlaw of the Feeney gang twitched convulsively in a pool of his own blood and gore. No one living moved for another stretched second.

Then Ki looked at the Captain, who nodded and said, "I'm not sure if that was stupid or crazy or plain old brave, Ki. But thanks for your help."

"You're welcome."

Cackling ripped the air. Ki spotted the old man waddling up to the dead outlaws.

"Well, Cap'n, deal's a deal."

"Go on. You've got two minutes. Sergeant, give this vulture two minutes, then hang these bodies over the extra mounts."

Ki moved back to his mount. He saw the big man in the white pants with the knife standing motionless at the end of the street. He looked like an Indian to Ki. Ki decided to find out what he wanted, if he was going to be following them around all day to report back to the General. Then the Indian disappeared around the corner.

Ki watched as the soldiers cleaned up the mess, urging the old man to pick up the pace. Nobody seemed to be paying any attention to him, so Ki decided to go off on his own mission.

He tethered his mount to the railing, then silently slipped away from the soldiers.

★

Chapter 9

Even though she was worried about Ki, Jessie had her own problems at the moment. The biggest problem she had right then was keeping the General's desire on a leash. If he touched her, he was dead, she determined, and she'd take her chances, fighting her way out of the palace with every bit of savage determination she could command. She knew Ki and the Captain would come back for her; she only hoped it wasn't too late when they returned.

A few minutes ago, she had heard the muffled din of weapons fire from beyond the walls of the palace. General Alfredo had sent a soldier out to investigate. It had sounded to her as if a savage but short battle had raged somewhere in the streets of San Pedro.

"I am a man of my word," the General told Jessie, then sucked down more pulque. "Should a citizen of San Pedro be hurt or killed by this Captain Frederick and his soldiers, then you will see me at my worst."

Jessie could believe that.

Time dragged. The General obviously wanted to keep the banquet table for himself and his "honored guest," as he referred to Jessie. Divans and smaller tables were clustered in corners of the hall for the General's other, obviously less important guests; the American *pistoleros*, the federales, and the whores. Jessie picked at some food, but she wasn't really hungry. The General tried to engage her in conversation, but she wasn't interested in the man or the stories he wanted to tell her about his past feats of bravery in battle. She answered whatever questions he put to her in monosyllabic grunting. He was trying to steer the conversation in the direction of a possible liaison between them. She ignored his sexual overtures, which only seemed to make him more insistent that they "amuse themselves to pass the time," as he put it. He was a braggart and a drunk, and he disgusted her.

And she also felt the eyes of every man in the room boring into her. The whores regarded her with resentment and jealousy. She expected trouble.

Trouble showed in the form of a white *pistolero*. He walked up to the banquet table, a bottle in his hand. He was drunk and he leered at Jessie.

"General, seems to me you got all the good stuff right up here," the *pistolero* said, slurring his words. "Somehow, that don't seem quite right. You need to learn how to share the wealth, General."

"Johnson, I have an honored guest here at my table. Show some respect."

Jessie tensed as Johnson walked up behind her. He was a tall, skinny gunman with long, stringy hair. He smelled to Jessie as if he hadn't bathed in years.

"Respect," Johnson snorted. "She's just another whore, General. I pay you good money. Least you can do is let me have a little fun with her. All the goddamn whores you got here smell and taste like shit. This *gringita* here looks like some fine sweet stuff. When I want something, General, I take it."

He bent to kiss Jessie, his free hand reaching out for her breast.

"Do not touch her!" the General barked.

Johnson wasn't about to listen, and he paid the ultimate price.

Jessie exploded into action. She threw out a backhand hammerfist, crushing Johnson's nose to bloody pulp. As he screamed and cursed, Jessie leapt to her feet. She speared a boot into his manhood, doubling him over. A terrible wail ripped from Johnson's mouth, his face twisted with agony.

The General laughed, and others in the banquet hall joined in his laughter. They were enjoying Johnson's misery, and Jessie wasn't surprised by their sadistic howling.

She wasn't finished with Johnson. She cracked his face with a savage open-palm slap, then grabbed a bottle off the table and smashed it over Johnson's head. Still he stood. And as he wobbled, rage in his eyes, Jessie craned a hook kick, a move that Ki had taught her, off his jaw, driving him into the wall. Johnson hit the floor on his rump. He shook his head like a wet dog, wiping the blood off his face with the back of his hand. Then a terrible rage filled his eyes.

"You bitch! I'll kill you!"

He reached for his revolver, but he never got the chance to use it. A shot rang out, and Johnson's chest was shredded to bloody tatters.

Jessie saw the smoking flintlock pistol in the General's hands.

"There," the General said. "That is what happens when someone treats my honored guests with disrespect. And, besides, he was a liar. His money was not that good." He then barked an order to one of his men to "remove this garbage from here." But they were to empty his pockets first, and any money they found they were to give to the General.

There were several moments of angry silence in the hall. Then the gunmen and the whores went back to drinking and groping one another.

The General looked at the body of Johnson as it was dragged off, then laughed. "I like the way you handle yourself. You are a tigress. I am hoping that before sundown you will, eh, loosen up and show me just what a tigress you are."

You bet I will, Jessie thought, but not in the way you think.

Moments later, a soldier ran up to the General and whispered something in his ear. He waved the man away.

"It would seem the Captain and his soldiers are hard at work," he told Jessie. "Your friend, he saved the lives of a woman and a young boy, I am told. Shall we, eh, say your luck is holding."

Jessie looked away from the General's leer and picked at some bread. She had to do something to get out of there, because she knew the General was not about to let her walk out at the appointed hour. Not without a fight. She tried not to look at her weapons, which had been left in a pile beside the General. She had to agree with him. At the moment, her luck was holding.

But when would her luck sour? she wondered. And just what was going on with Ki at the moment?

As Jessie was proving herself a tigress to be reckoned with, Ki was walking the streets of San Pedro alone. Again, one block over from the cantina, he spotted the Indian with the big knife. And again the Indian appeared to be shadowing his every move, Ki thought, but his shadow kept about a half-block distance between them. Followed or stalked? Ki wondered.

He moved down an alley. He peeked into an open doorway and found the small room deserted. He ducked into the room and waited. Moments later he saw a big shadow falling over the doorway. With a lightning attack he reached out, fisted a handful of the Indian's hair, and dragged him into the room, hurling him to the floor.

"You're following me!" Ki said. "Why?"

"You die! Guamo will slice you open and wrap your guts around your neck. I will take your body back to the General to piss on!"

The knife came out of the Indian's sash, and he charged Ki. Ki swept a hook-kick off the Indian's jaw. Bone pounded bone with a crack, and Guamo stumbled deeper into the shadows of the room.

Ki unsheathed his *katana*. Guamo hesitated for a second, staring at the curved sword, then laughed. He swished his blade, back and forth, closing on Ki. Ki swung the sword for a decapitating blow, but Guamo ducked. Guamo lashed out at Ki's midsection, but Ki danced back as the blade swiped at air. With a furious attack, Guamo rushed Ki, his blade a blur as he slashed at Ki's face and head. Ki couldn't get close enough to use his sword, as Guamo backed him up against the wall. Guamo took a swipe at Ki's head, but the blade slammed into the wall. The force of the blade hitting the wall seemed to stun Guamo with bone-jarring pain. It was a critical split second in hesitation that Ki used to his deadly advantage.

Ki drove his sword through Guamo's ribs. A look of shock and horror etched itself into Guamo's face as blood streamed from the wound in his side. Ki slid the blade free from Guamo. The knife slipped from Guamo's hand, and he toppled, ramrod stiff, to the floor, staring up at the ceiling with wide, lifeless eyes. Guamo died with a look of utter disbelief on his face. Ki wiped his blade off on Guamo's pants and sheathed his sword. He worried about the body being found. If, in fact, the General had sent this Guamo out after him, then Ki was afraid he would hold Jessie hostage in return for some kind of sick favor or deadly justice. Time was running out in San Pedro, Ki knew, and total war might not wait until sundown to break out.

Ki checked the doorway. At the moment, no one appeared to be on the narrow street in front of the door where Ki had just won a life-and-death encounter.

He hit the street, heading back in the direction of the cantina where Captain Frederick and his soldiers had slaughtered the Feeney gang.

He was prepared to round the corner when he heard, "Whoa, look what we got here, fellas."

A chill went down Ki's spine. He turned and found the bounty hunters on horseback, right behind him.

Jake Kingston grinned from ear to ear. "So, I see you made it. Guess the Cap'n's a little unhappy about us takin' off like we did. And with his dynamite."

Ki tensed, prepared to draw if the bounty hunters went for their weapons, but they didn't reach for iron.

"You could say that," Ki said.

"Well, we heard the Cap'n's here. Already caused quite a stir. Fact, he probably killed a few wanted men that rightfully belong to us. Well, you can go back to the Cap'n, boy. Tell him to stay out of our way, 'cause I got enough dynamite here to level all a San Pedro."

"Might be best if you made yourself scarce, Kingston," Ki said. "You don't have enough men to take on the Captain and the federales at the same time."

"We'll see about that."

And Ki left the bounty hunters to do whatever it was they were going to do. Minutes later he was back at the cantina, where the Captain had hog-tied the bodies of the outlaws over the extra horses.

"Where the hell have you been?" the Captain demanded.

"Getting someone off our backs," Ki told him.

"What's that supposed to mean?"

"It means there's going to be serious trouble, Captain. I suggest we do something about the situation at the palace before it's too late. Worse, I just ran into the bounty hunters."

"All right, we run into them, I'll deal with them, the same way we just dealt with Feeney and his bunch."

"I don't think it's going to be that easy, Captain."

"We'll see about that."

Ki chuckled, a grim sound. "Funny, that's what Jake Kingston just told me."

Another eternal hour passed. Jessie watched in mounting anxiety as the General became drunker and drunker and his overtures took on obscene tones. His head swayed from side to side and drool ran from the corner of his mouth. There had been more sounds of gunfire beyond the palace wall, echoing from somewhere in the distance. San Pedro appeared to be a city under siege. If the General was concerned about his city, he didn't show it around Jessie.

A soldier reported to the General.

"It would seem," the General said, after dismissing his underling, "that your Captain is still hard at work. And there are other gringos in San Pedro. Killing more gringos. I am told they are bounty hunters. San Pedro is becoming too crowded with fortune seekers. I will have to demand a cut of all profits from blood money."

The situation was about to explode. Jessie could feel the General becoming more volatile with each passing minute. She had to do something. The only way out of San Pedro was going to be a savage fighting withdrawal, she knew.

"When the gringos are done having their fun, they will come back here. But, they will deal with me. I am not prepared to let you go so easy. Not until I get all which is owed me."

The General snapped his fingers, demanding another bottle.

Jessie felt her heart race with fear. Soon, very soon, she would have to make some kind of wild grandstand play. She only hoped that at the decisive moment in which she decided to act, Ki and Captain Frederick would burst through the doors. If she were forced to fight on her own, it could well prove to be her final few moments of life.

Ki had run out of patience. "Captain, I'm going back to the General's palace to demand he hand Jessie over. Either you're with me or you're not. If you're not with me on this at this very moment, then I'll do whatever it is I have to do to get Jessie out of there."

They had hunted down another dozen outlaws and been forced to kill them. They had marched into cantinas and combed buildings and shot it out with outlaws who had opted to go down fighting rather than face arrest. Ki had not participated in any of the executions. All he could think about was Jessie.

"Come on, Captain," Ki urged. "You've got a lot of what you came for, damn it. Aren't you concerned about Jessie?"

A hard look fell over the Captain's face. Two more dead outlaws were being hog-tied to extra mounts. The Captain mounted his horse. The sun was beginning to set over San Pedro, long shadows stretching over the narrow, congested streets. Many of the Mexicans who lived here had apparently opted to go into hiding. And the streets were now almost deserted. During the hunting, Ki had seen federales watching the action from a distance. He worried about the body of Guamo being discovered.

"All right, Ki. The sun's almost down. Which means our time is up."

"Fine. But something tells me, Captain, that the General is not going to just hand Jessie over."

"Then we march right in and demand he do it at gunpoint. You ready for that?"

"I've been ready, Captain."

"You insult me, *gringita*."

Jessie looked at the General. There was cold fury in his eyes.

"How do I insult you, General? I have said nothing to offend you."

He was about to answer, looked set to explode in a violent tantrum, when a soldier ran up to him and whispered something in his ear. Jessie would have thought all the whispering that was taking place in the General's ear comical if the situation hadn't been such a powderkeg.

"It would seem someone has killed Guamo." The General's voice cracked with rage. "It would appear he was killed by an instrument resembling a knife, or a sword perhaps. Your friend, he had such a weapon." He paused. "How do you insult me? I tell you. It is not what you have said or not said. It is what you have not done. For me. I give you food, I offer you drink, I give you my home. I let your gringo friends roam my city and kill the men they came here for at will. Now I feel insulted by the whole situation; I have lost all patience. I am insulted by the mere fact that your government would even come to Mexico and demand their own criminals. And yet I get nothing in return. You treat me like I am some . . . insect. You sit there; I can tell you despise me. You are nothing but a whore! I have waited long enough." He snapped his fingers, and two federales with rifles ran up to the table.

Jessie felt cold fear ripple through her chest.

The General stood and barked, "Come here to me. Now!"

★

Chapter 10

The clop of hooves filled Ki's ears and dust choked his senses as they rounded the corner, marching onto the wide street that led to the General's palace. Ki was prepared to fight to the death to save Jessie.

He wasn't prepared to have to fight it out with the bounty hunters.

But several of the bounty hunters stood in their way, halfway down the street.

The Captain called the march to a halt.

Ki looked at Jake Kingston, who was standing beside three dead men, grinning over their outstretched bodies. Ki saw only three other bounty hunters, and they were standing several yards behind Kingston, rifles in hand. He wondered where the others were. Maybe waiting in ambush? Were they that crazy? Less than ten men willing to take on forty-plus soldiers? Whatever, Ki suspected trouble, and he would soon discover just how much of a threat the bounty hunters posed. Nearby a large buckboard, drawn by two geldings, was loaded with bodies. Ki watched as

Kingston jerked a nod at the dead men at his feet and the bounty hunters heaved the corpses into the buckboard.

"Mister, I am placing you under arrest," the Captain announced.

Under the circumstances, Ki thought that was a damn dumb thing to say. Obviously Jake Kingston thought the same thing.

"For what?"

"For stealing the property of the United States Army."

Kingston laughed, scratched a match off the heel of his boot, and fired up a cigar. "Speaking of that property, Cap'n, I've got some of it for you." He jerked a nod to his left, indicating a cantina. "It's in there. Care to get it?"

"What the hell's the meaning of this?" Captain Frederick demanded.

"It means we've got a problem, that only you can solve. You see, inside there, I've got three bundles of dynamite ready to go off, I give the word. Be a shame. There's about a dozen women and children inside. All of them scared to death, blubbering and weeping and gnashing their teeth. Hey, don't get me wrong, I'm not some man without a heart here. But only you, Cap'n, can determine what will happen to them."

Ki felt cold rage in the pit of his belly. If it had been up to him, he would have shot Jake Kingston where he stood. But the bounty hunter held all the cards. At least for the moment.

"What do you want?"

Kingston took several deep, leisurely puffs off his cigar, blew out clouds of smoke. "What I want, Cap'n, is that booty you got hog-tied there to them mounts. They belong to me. Those dead men are money in my pocket, and you ain't gonna take money outta my hand. You don't hand them over . . . well, like I said, I give the word, I blow up this cantina. Be innocent blood on your hands, Cap'n. I know you're a man of conscience. I know you can't let that happen."

"You rotten bastard," Sergeant Milrose snarled, reaching for his revolver.

"Sergeant!" the Captain barked. "Stay your hand."

"Well, Cap'n? What's the deal here? Dead men for live Mexicans? You pick it. C'mon, Cap'n, somethin' tells me that if greaser blood gits spilled, all hell's gonna break loose and the General's gonna send his guns after you. You won't make it outta San Pedro alive that happens."

Ki saw the Captain hesitate. The Captain cursed. During the past couple of hours, Ki had heard shooting from somewhere in San Pedro. He couldn't tell how many dead men were piled in the buckboard, but the bounty hunters had obviously been hard at work.

"Cap'n. I'm waiting. Don't tell me what we got here is a Mexican standoff. That's the case, you'll lose. All you got to do is hand over those dead men and let us ride out of San Pedro."

"Captain, do what he wants," Ki urged. "You've got innocent lives hanging in the balance."

The Captain waited a long moment before answering. "Sergeant, send those dead men down to this scumsucker."

"Now, now, Cap'n, no need to be calling me

names," Kingston said, and laughed.

Sergeant Milrose cursed, then rounded up several soldiers. They led the mounts carrying dead outlaws toward the bounty hunters.

"Much obliged, Cap'n."

Ki detected some note of treachery in Kingston's voice. Something warned him that Kingston was not going to live up to his end of the bargain.

"Now, you wait until we're outta your sight, Cap'n," Kingston said. "Then you can proceed."

The bodies of outlaws the Army had accumulated were tossed into the buckboard. Ki couldn't hear what Sergeant Milrose said to Kingston, but he heard Kingston tell the sergeant to be a good little bootlicker and get the hell on back.

"I say we open fire on them, Captain," Sergeant Milrose said when he returned and mounted.

"I say we'll catch up to them later," the Captain replied. "Now isn't the time."

The rest of the bounty hunters strode out of the cantina, dynamite in their hands. A bounty hunter climbed onto the seat of the buckboard and led the dead man's wagon around the corner. Suddenly, without warning, Kingston lit his bundle of dynamite and hurled it at the soldiers, while two other bounty hunters lit their bundles and tossed them into the cantina.

Jessie knew the General was not going to be denied. What he didn't know, she thought, was that he had just left her with no choice but to kill him and fight her way out of the palace.

They had not bothered to frisk her, so her derringer was still tucked behind her belt buckle.

But she needed to get to her revolver. Either the General had been careless or he thought himself so invincible that a lone woman wouldn't dare make a dash to get her gun. His arrogance, Jessie determined, would be his final undoing.

The General trembled with fury. "Come here, I said! Or my men will drag you to me and force you on your knees before me!"

Jessie hesitated, looking at the two soldiers in front of the table. They had not aimed their rifles at her yet, which might give her a precious split second to get her revolver. She decided to put on a seductive act, appear to be ready to give the General what he wanted. He might see through her act, he might not, she thought, but her time was up.

"Okay, General, I'll do whatever you wish. You're a handsome man. I've decided, Why not?"

The General looked stunned for a moment, then an oily smile slid over his lips as Jessie slowly walked up to him.

She kept the soldiers in the corner of her eye. She moved in front of the General, keeping him between her and the soldiers. She moistened her lips with the tip of her tongue, staring the General dead in the eye. He licked his own lips, his stare burning with desire and anticipation. Jessie was prepared to push him back into his soldiers, go for her gun, and go for broke.

Then, suddenly, several loud explosions thundered from beyond the palace walls, and terrible screams sounded from somewhere nearby. A panic went through the banquet hall. The General and his soldiers looked toward the doorway.

And Jessie made her move.

With fear-powered rage, she shoved the General into his soldiers. As the General and his men toppled to the floor, Jessie scooped up her holster. The General shrieked a curse, but it was the last thing he ever said.

Sliding her Colt free from its holster, Jessie shot the General in the forehead, then turned her aim on the two soldiers. They froze for a critical heartbeat in utter shock, as their General's blood washed over them. With two lightning rounds, Jessie ended their profound confusion, drilling one shot each into their chests.

But the battle had only just begun, Jessie discovered.

Soldiers from across the hall were screaming curses at her. Jessie threw her shoulder into the banquet table, hurling it up on its side, plates of food and bottles of pulque flying through the air. With catlike grace, she ducked behind it as bullets began tattooing the wood. She fixed a grim stare on the door through which the Grimm gang had entered and left the hall. It was her only way out. She was only one gun against dozens of enraged soldiers and frightened gringo *pistoleros.*

Jessie bolted from cover, returning fire, as bullets whined off the wall beside her. She reached the door, threw it open, and ran down the narrow passageway. She had no idea what was at the end of the corridor, but she was braced for the worst. Quickly, on the run, she reloaded her revolver.

Chaos, confusion, and death choked the streets of San Pedro.

Ki veered his mount away from the dynamite bundle, racing for the corner of the closest building.

The cantina was blown into the sky by a series of tremendous blasts. Nothing and no one, Ki knew, would survive those explosions inside the cantina.

Many of Captain Frederick's soldiers, packed tightly together in the middle of the street, were not as fortunate as Ki. The sticks blew, halfway down the line of soldiers, shredding man and animal alike.

As rubble pelted the street, and bits and pieces of flesh rained to earth, screams of pain and rage and fear ripped the air, Ki urged his mount into the billowing clouds of dust and cordite. Why the bounty hunters had done what they had, Ki could only guess. Maybe it was some form of twisted revenge on the Captain. Maybe they wanted to create mayhem to cover their escape from San Pedro. Maybe they were just plain crazy. Whatever, they had created a situation from which no gringo might emerge alive. Innocent blood had been shed, and the Mexican people of San Pedro would demand retribution.

There was now no sign of the bounty hunters down the adjacent street. They had made a clean getaway. Ki seethed. He vowed their day would come and they would answer to him.

But first he had to get to Jessie.

Ki spotted a broken-open crate of dynamite that had fallen from one of the bounty hunter's horses in his haste to flee. He dismounted, holding his panicky mount tightly by the reins, scooped up several sticks, and tucked them inside his waistband.

"Ki! Wait!"

As he mounted, Ki spotted Captain Frederick riding out of the roiling smoke. Ki had no time to wait. The General would have heard the explosions, perhaps even secured a perimeter around the palace with his men. Ahead, Ki spotted federales pouring through the front doors, armed to the teeth.

It was going to take all-out war to get inside the palace, Ki knew.

Weaving his way through riderless horses scrambling pell-mell all over the street, Ki charged the palace, the Captain and a dozen soldiers right on his heels. Unsheathing his Winchester, Ki dismounted and crouched behind a low wall that ran in front of the courtyard. His Winchester bucked and flamed, again and again. He struck lethal pay dirt three times, and he took some grim satisfaction in watching three federales spin and plunge down the short flight of steps that led to the main foyer. Captain Frederick and his soldiers dismounted, taking up positions beside Ki.

More federales appeared on the front porch.

As return fire peppered the wall, showering stone over their heads, Ki told the Captain, "We have to go in. There's only one way. And that's charge the palace!"

Striking a match off his boot heel, Ki lit a stick of dynamite. He hurled the dynamite at the soldiers on the steps. As the stick detonated, catapulting shredded figures in every direction,

Ki raced across the courtyard. He only hoped he was in time to save Jessie. And if he couldn't save her, he thought, he would at least die fighting by her side.

Her holster secured around her waist, Jessie came out of the passageway to find herself in the main foyer. She looked to her side and saw she was at the foot of a flight of steps that led to the second floor.

She also came under fire from the Grimm gang.

As she ducked behind the wall, a split second before a lead barrage swarmed over her position, she heard Judd Grimm screaming curses at her, how she had ruined everything and he was going to make her pay dearly. She looked down the hall, toward the open front doors. Just then, Ki and Captain Frederick and a dozen or so of his soldiers hit the steps. Federales and American *pistoleros* were pouring out of the banquet hall, but they were greeted by instant death. Ki, the Captain, and his soldiers directed a relentless stream of lead toward the banquet-hall doorway. Bullet-riddled men, both in and out of uniform, were pounded backward into the hall, dancing jigs of death, soaking one another with their blood as it sprayed the air.

In the next instant, crouched and chancing a look around the corner, Jessie saw Judd Grimm go for his best ploy.

The stick of dynamite bounced right in front of her. The fuse had sizzled down to a quarter inch. It was crazy, she knew, but she was fighting for her life. Firing around the corner at the eight outlaws at the top of the steps, Jessie swept up the dynamite bundle.

Ki must've seen what she did, because he shouted, "Jessie! No!"

Jessie flung the dynamite stick up the steps.

Judd Grimm's eyes widened with terror. And the Grimm gang scrambled away from the dynamite, bumping into each other as they tried to run down the second-story hall.

Behind Jessie, bodies kept piling up in the banquet-hall doorway.

Ki and Captain Frederick and his soldiers burst into the foyer, firing for all they were worth.

And the dynamite stick blew at the top of the steps. Jessie flung herself behind the cover of the wall as rubble showered down on the foyer. If any of the Grimm gang had survived the blast, she intended to find out. She broke cover, as Ki ran beside the Captain and his soldiers. Captain Frederick and his men charged into the banquet hall. The din of weapons fire was deafening.

"Jessie! Wait!" Ki shouted.

But Jessie plunged into the cordite. A bloody figure wobbled at the top of the steps, aiming a revolver at her. She shot the figure twice in the chest, flinging him back across the second-story hall.

She topped the steps, searching the smoke-choked hall in both directions. Nothing moved. She counted up the shredded remains of two bodies, including the gang member she had just shot. Only two? she thought. Damn. The rest of the Grimm gang had survived to kill another day.

Then she heard sharp groaning and ventured down the hall toward the source of that sound of pain. Below her, the bark of weapons went on and on.

As she cleared the smoke, moving cautiously down the hall, she couldn't believe what she found. Outstretched beneath her were both Judd and Eli Grimm. With dazed looks, clearly on the verge of lapsing into unconsciousness, they stared up at Jessie.

★

Chapter 11

As the Captain and his men waged their own battle against the outlaws in the banquet hall, Ki, Winchester in hand, bounded up the steps for the second floor. Wild-eyed, he searched the hallway for outlaws, but found nothing moving in either direction. Then he ran up beside Jessie, who was standing over the Grimm brothers. After the blast he had seen sweep the second-story hall, it was incredible to Ki that they were even still alive.

"The rest of them escaped?" Ki asked, incredulous.

Judd Grimm chuckled. "Lady Luck's always smiled on the Grimm gang, boy."

"Not for long," Jessie told the outlaw.

Ki saw an open door beside him. Carefully, he moved into the large bedroom.

Across the bedroom he saw an open window. Beyond it he heard the pounding of hooves. When he reached the window, he saw four men on horseback, racing away from San Pedro, heading north. He would have shot them off their mounts, but they were already well out of the firing range of his rifle. He cursed the luck of the Grimm gang.

Back out in the hall, Ki heard Judd Grimm telling Jessie, "Go on, bitch. Shoot me. Get it over with."

Ki saw the rage flash through Jessie's green eyes and knew she was considering honoring the outlaw's request. She hesitated, then shook her head.

"No," she told Judd Grimm in a cold voice. "A quick death is too good for the likes of you. I have a better idea. I don't care what it takes, but you two are going back across the border."

"For what?" Eli Grimm said, then groaned in pain.

"To stand trial in the town of Goodwill," Jessie told them. "For murder."

"No way will you get us back there alive just so you can watch us hang," Judd Grimm rasped.

"We'll see about that. Ki, I need something to tie their hands up with."

"The rest of this bunch escaped, Jessie," Ki said.

Judd Grimm laughed. "And they'll be out there. Waiting. Believe me, a lot of bad things can happen between here and Goodwill."

Ki moved to the tattered remains of an outlaw. He took the hunting knife off the corpse, then cut thick strips of his pant leg off. Judd Grimm tried to stand and charge Jessie, but Ki descended on him, driving a short, chopping right off his jaw and knocking him on his back.

"You want some of that, too?" he asked Eli Grimm.

"Go to hell."

"No, that's where you're going," Ki said. "Eventually."

"Move, and I'll shoot you in the leg," Jessie told Eli Grimm. "Better tie their hands in front of them, Ki, so they can ride."

Quickly, Ki secured the hands of both outlaws. Then he roughly hauled both outlaws to their feet. Judd Grimm complained of a ringing in his ears, said he thought he might pass out.

"Payback's hell, isn't it?" Ki told him. "I hope it hurts every time you breathe."

Ki found a lot of desperate activity down in the foyer. Gunshots sounded from beyond the palace, and Ki knew more trouble waited for all of them. Hastily, soldiers were leading mounts through the doorway and into the foyer, as bullets ricocheted off the doorway or blasted out the front windows. Keeping the Grimm brothers between them, Jessie and Ki descended the steps. Quickly, the hallway was packed with soldiers and horses. It looked to Ki as if the Captain's number of soldiers was down to about two dozen, maybe thirty, uniforms.

"What's going on, Captain?" Jessie asked.

"Looks like we've got about twenty, maybe thirty, federales outside, angry as a stirred-up hornet's nest," the Captain told her. He looked at Jessie for a moment, then added, "I'm glad you're all right, Jessie."

"Well, we're not clear and free of anything yet, Captain," she said.

"Do tell. Last thing we need is to get pinned down and surrounded. What's with these two? Are they . . ."

"The Grimm brothers, Judd and Eli," Jessie said.

"I thought you wanted to see them dead?"

"I changed my mind, Captain. A lady's prerogative, right? Instead, I want to take them back to Goodwill. The people of that town have a right to decide their fate."

"First, we have to get out of here," the Captain pointed out, "then get back across the border, hoping that half the Mexican Army isn't nipping at our heels."

Soldiers were crouched beside the front doorway, returning fire, rifles and revolvers blazing lead at the federales across the courtyard. For several more seconds the doorway continued to be peppered with bullets; then a voice, speaking in Spanish, boomed from somewhere outside. The shooting stopped.

"You, in there, gringos! I am *Capitán* Juan Suarez of the federales. You are surrounded!"

Captain Frederick ordered ten soldiers to secure the back of the building and shoot anything that tried to charge the palace from the rear.

The Captain, Ki, and Jessie flanked the open doorway. Ki counted about twenty uniformed Mexicans beyond the low wall. Clouds of gunsmoke hung over the courtyard. From behind Ki, Judd Grimm chuckled.

"Don't look like nobody's gonna get outta San Pee-dro alive. Sir."

"Shut your mouth!" Captain Frederick snapped at the outlaw.

"If my memory serves me correct," Captain Juan Suarez continued, "we are not at war with your country. I believe thees is perhaps a violation of some treaty, no? American soldiers coming here to Mexico and killing Mexican citizens. I find it dee-fee-cult to believe your government would permit such a thing."

"We didn't kill those people in the cantina, Captain," Captain Frederick shouted through the doorway. "The men who blew up that cantina with those women and children inside, believe me, I want them every bit as bad as you."

"But you are the cause. Were it not for you, I must believe they would not have been here. They escaped. You are here. Someone has to take the blame. I have come many miles from my post in San Miguel when I heard American soldiers were in San Pedro, killing. I know General Alfredo is a corrupt pig of a man and he would not stand up to you. He loves only his drink and his whores and his gold, he is no true *soldado*. No *cajones*. Is not so with me. You will surrender or you will die."

"*Was* a corrupt pig of a man," Jessie said.

Captain Frederick looked at Jessie. "So, you settled at least one score."

"I mean what I say! Look!" Captain Suarez shouted.

Ki looked over the shoulder of Captain Frederick, watching the action outside. Two soldiers hauled Sergeant Milrose up to the courtyard wall and thrust him to his knees beside Captain Suarez, who was a short, stocky federale with a uniform that appeared to be laden with medals.

"Don't surrender, Captain, don't give these bastards an inch . . ."

Then, as if to prove his point, Captain Suarez unholstered a pistol and shot Sergeant Milrose in the head.

"You bastard." Captain Frederick seethed.

"I give you ten minutes, Captain!"

An escape plan formed in Ki's mind. "Captain, can I make a suggestion on how we get out of here?"

"Make it quick. Our time's up. Take a look at that."

Just then, hearing the creak and groan of leather and metal, Ki saw three horses, each horse drawing a cannon up to the courtyard wall.

"Ten minutes, then I blow thees place down around your heads!"

A grim smile cut Ki's lips. "Well, Captain, you know what I think?"

"What?"

"Coming to San Pedro has definitely put a strain on U.S.–Mexican relations. Unfortunately, the only way out of here is to strain those relations even more."

The plan was simple but dangerous, and Jessie feared more soldiers would lose their lives in the battle that was most certainly just minutes away. Not to mention the danger to herself and Ki, who had insisted on being responsible for launching the fighting retreat. But the Captain had agreed to Ki's plan as the only way out of the palace. Hurl dynamite at the federales, who had taken up positions at the rear of the palace, and make a run for it across the wide open area to the northeast. Even if they made it beyond the palace grounds, Jessie

119

knew it was going to be a long and grueling and dangerous race for the border. The federales were going to dog them all the way to the Rio Grande. It was too late to worry about any diplomatic relations with Mexico. The damage had been done.

Behind Jessie, the horses had been strung out in a line down the hall. Because of the lack of them, some soldiers would be forced to double up in the saddle. Just inside the open patio doorway, Jessie stood near the front of the line, with Ki and Captain Frederick beside her. The soldiers who had volunteered to be the first out of the doorway were ahead of Jessie, already mounted up, their revolvers drawn. And the Grimm brothers were mounted also, but the Captain had ordered their hands to be bound more securely with rope. Jessie had already warned the brothers that if they made a break for freedom during the ensuing fighting withdrawal, she would shoot them in the legs. She meant business: They were going back to Goodwill, alive.

Captain Frederick was checking the grounds behind the palace, and Jessie sized up the odds also. Perhaps fifteen federales, crouched with rifles behind a low-running wall to the north, positioned less than fifty feet from the patio doorway and were mere shadows beneath the setting sun. Jessie looked at Ki, who held four sticks of twined dynamite in his hand.

"It's a damn good thing your lieutenant thought to grab a few more of those dynamite sticks off the street," Ki told the Captain. "We're going to need all the dynamite we have. We hit and run and hope for the best, Captain."

"Jessie, stay to my right flank," the Captain said.

"I can handle myself, Captain. If a stray bullet gets me, well, it gets me. We're all in the same amount of danger."

The Captain didn't look pleased with Jessie's response, but he turned away from her and nodded at Ki. "Let's do it."

Jessie mounted up and unholstered her revolver. She told the Grimm brothers, "You two stay beside me. Remember what I said."

"Hey, bitch, we'll do it your way," Judd Grimm said. "Some life is better than no life."

"I'll keep that in mind for you," Jessie said. "Right now, your lives belong to me."

A match flared in Ki's hand, and he lit the dynamite sticks and ran out onto the patio. As he hurled the dynamite toward the federales, the first few American soldiers broke cover, revolvers blazing in their hands. The federales cut loose with a volley of rifle fire, and two more of Captain Frederick's men toppled from their mounts, dead before they hit the ground, bloody, twitching meat for the buzzards.

"Move!" Jessie roared at the Grimm brothers.

Ki mounted and urged his horse ahead and across the patio, to race beside Jessie and the Grimm brothers.

The sticks blew, and several tremendous explosions ripped through the firing line of federales. Mangled bodies were launched over the wall on raging tongues of fire. Horribly wounded men began screaming like banshees as stone shrapnel tore through them.

121

Jessie dug her heels into the flanks of her horse, demanding more speed. Suddenly she heard cannon fire from behind her. With one eye on the Grimm brothers, who were doing as she had told them, she saw smoke billow through the patio doorway and heard more screaming of men in terrible agony. Soldiers in the rear of the hallway, she knew, had just been hit by cannon fire.

But one by one, American soldiers kept pouring through the patio doorway, firing with revolvers at a few federales who had survived the dynamite blasts.

Jessie heard more cannon fire thunder from behind her. As she veered her mount to the northeast, she aimed her Colt at the Grimm brothers and shouted, "This way!"

Then Ki rode up on the right flank of the brothers, one hand on the reins, the Remington in his other hand.

Captain Frederick took the lead, racing his mount toward the hills to the north of San Pedro.

"Now what, Captain?" Ki shouted.

"I don't know, but I'll think of something."

Jessie looked behind her, toward San Pedro, as Captain Frederick led them into a gorge that cut through the hills. A long spool of dust trailed the federales. The fighting withdrawal, she knew, was far from over.

"Hold up!" the Captain ordered his troops.

The soldiers reined in their mounts. The Captain stared out across the plain at the federales racing their way. Then he looked down the gorge.

It cut all the way through the hills, but it became apparent in the next moment that the Captain was going to stand his ground and fight it out with the federales.

"Everyone, move into this gorge, dismount, and take up positions on both sides. Fire only on my order!"

Ki spoke up. "Captain, if you can draw them in, I can backtrack and hit them from the rear with dynamite."

It took but a second for the Captain to make his decision. "Lieutenant Hankins, give him the rest of that dynamite."

Ki took the dynamite. Then the Captain gave him a cigar.

"If you're not a smoking man, I suggest now might be the time to start," the Captain said. "At least it'll make it easier to light those sticks. Let's move out!"

★

Chapter 12

With Captain Frederick and his troops, Jessie rode deeper into the gorge, listening to the distant thunder of hoofbeats behind her, knowing that all of them were either going to die there, shooting it out with the federales, or free themselves of their Mexican hunters for good. She looked at Judd Grimm, who was grinning, as if he was savoring some private joke. She couldn't believe what she was seeing. The outlaw actually appeared to be on the verge of laughing out loud.

"You're enjoying this, aren't you?" Jessie said. "You're a sick bastard."

Judd Grimm shrugged. "That's right, I'm a sick bastard. An' so what? If me and my brother gonna die anyway, ain't nothin' gonna please me more, bitch, than to watch you and the half-breed get yours from them goddamn greasers."

Brother Judd might have been smug about his predicament, but Eli Grimm looked clearly afraid to Jessie. Then, as Captain Frederick ordered his troops to dismount and take up their positions, Eli Grimm made a sudden break for freedom. But

Jessie caught him within several quick strides of her mount and clipped him over the head with her revolver, knocking him from the saddle. She swung her aim toward Judd Grimm, who cursed her.

"Off the horse. Now! Either of you tries to run again, I swear I'll shoot you in the leg. Then I'll bind the wound myself and throw you back on the saddle. I meant what I said. You're going back to Goodwill to stand trial."

As the soldiers were herding the horses into a narrow gulley, Captain Frederick dismounted and marched up to Jessie.

"If we get out of here, Jessie," the Captain said, "these two might prove more trouble than they're worth."

After dropping off her mount, Jessie hustled the two outlaws several yards up the side of the gorge at gunpoint. "I'm willing to take my chances with them, Captain."

"So you won't reconsider just shooting them dead if they try and run again?" the Captain asked.

"Let's take care of this problem we have with the federales first, then I might leave myself open to any suggestions you have regarding these two," Jessie said, watching as the soldiers took up positions behind boulders on both sides of the gorge. She looked up and found Ki, crouched and moving for higher ground.

"You ain't got the guts to kill us in cold blood," Judd Grimm taunted.

"Maybe, maybe not. But are you really willing to find out?"

Then Jessie was forced to turn her attention toward the front of the gorge, as the federales appeared over the rise.

"Here," Captain Frederick said, tossing Jessie a Winchester rifle. "We picked up some extra weapons on the way out of the palace. Wait until they're well into the gorge. I'll give the order when to fire."

Jessie saw Judd Grimm suddenly open his mouth, as if to shout a warning at the federales. She jammed the muzzle of her Colt into his ear and cocked the hammer.

"Some life is better than no life," she said. "Isn't that what you said?"

Those words and the stone-cold look in Jessie's eyes shut Judd Grimm's mouth.

From his vantage point overlooking the gorge, Ki watched as the federales moved into the gorge. Perhaps a little more than halfway down the gorge, Ki spotted the American soldiers, crouched behind boulders or outstretched in prone positions in gulleys, with rifles poised to fire. They appeared to be hidden from the federales, but he couldn't be sure.

Ki had ten sticks of dynamite, tucked inside his gunbelt. Laying his Winchester on the ground, he took three of the sticks in hand, his grim stare fixed on the federales. They were maybe a hundred feet directly below him now. He had been told to wait until the Captain and his troops opened fire. Ki's part in the ambush was to take out as many of the federales as he could with the first few sticks, then hit them from the rear and drive them into the guns of Captain Frederick and his men.

At first, it didn't appear that the federales suspected an ambush. Then Captain Suarez raised his hand, a silent signal for his thirty-strong force to halt. They were just inside the mouth of the gorge, and they were grouped close together. Perfect, Ki thought. He was going to be able to knock out quite a few of their number right away. For several stretched seconds, Captain Suarez stared down the gorge.

As quietly as possible, leaning away from the edge, Ki struck a match off his boot heel and fired up the cigar. He felt his heart pounding, faster and faster, with each passing moment. If they looked up and spotted the smoke now, Ki knew he'd have to start the battle alone.

It was bad luck that tipped off the Mexicans and started the battle.

Several of the horses that had been hidden in the gully by Captain Frederick's men whinnied, alerting the federales to the trap.

Captain Suarez began shouting orders in Spanish, his voice shrill with panic as his men started to dismount.

"Fire!"

A deafening hail of rifle fire erupted from the American soldiers.

Ki lit the dynamite.

Some of the federales managed to dismount and race for cover, but several were blown out of their saddles by the initial lead onslaught.

As soon as Ki hurled the three sticks of dynamite down into the dust storm being whipped up by the federales and their mounts, he plucked two more sticks free and lit them with the glowing tip of his cigar. Below Ki, the triple blasts ripped through the Mexicans, scything man and animal apart, spreading severed limbs and hurling broken bodies across the gorge.

Dynamite blasts and hellish swarms of lead had given the Americans the initial advantage. But it quickly became obvious to Ki that the federales were going to fight down to the last man.

The American soldiers poured it on the Mexicans with a relentless barrage of bullets. A half-dozen federales never made it to cover, as they were cut down by the ferocious, tracking streams of lead. Shredded by bullets, those federales caught out in the open screamed, spun, and toppled to the floor of the gorge.

Ki pitched two more sticks below him, aiming them for a group of about six Mexicans who had had the misfortune to choose his side of the gorge for cover. The twin explosions decimated the enemy numbers even more. Ki pitched another sizzling stick to the rear of the federales, where several of them were retreating for the mouth of the gorge. The resultant thundering fireball did exactly what Ki had hoped for, which was to drive the surviving federales back into the gorge as they realized they were being hit from the rear.

Now the Mexicans were pinched in by attacks from the rear and the front. For them there was no escape; there were only the waiting arms of death.

Ki let fly with one more stick, then grabbed up his rifle and began picking off federales wherever they ran. One man pointed up at Ki's position, and Ki shot him in the face.

Sporadic return fire was being directed at the American soldiers by the few surviving federales dug into pockets at the mouth of the gorge. When the shooting had started and Ki had gone to work with the dynamite, Jessie had done her part, firing away with her Winchester and dropping two federales. Only seconds ago, two soldiers beside her had died from Mexican bullets to the chest. When they fell in death, Judd Grimm had laughed. As she fired at the federales with her Winchester, Jessie was still seething about the outlaw's utter lack of humanity. Now, more than ever, she was determined to see the brothers hang in Goodwill.

Suddenly the federales stopped shooting. Voices, speaking in Spanish, echoed down the gorge. Jessie lowered her rifle. She looked at Captain Frederick, who was clutching his own smoking Winchester, a look of suspicion on his face.

"Hold your fire!" the Captain ordered as six, then seven federales slowly stepped into the middle of the gorge, their hands raised in the air.

"We surrender! *No mas!*"

Jessie spotted Ki, standing atop the ridge of the gorge. He covered the surviving Mexicans with his Winchester.

"Are there any more survivors?" Captain Frederick called out.

"No," came the solemn reply from one of federales.

"Shoot the greaser shits, Cap'n!" Judd Grimm urged.

Cold rage filled the Captain's eyes. "Shut your mouth, mister. One more word out of you and I'll beat you half to death."

Flanked by several of his soldiers, the Captain walked toward the federales. One eye on the Grimm brothers, Jessie watched and listened.

"What's your name, soldier?"

"I am Miguel Ramirez."

"Okay, soldier," the Captain said. "I want to tell you this, so that when you go back to your post, there's no misunderstanding. I did not want this to happen. We did not come down here to start a war with your country. Innocent people died in San Pedro. We did not kill them."

"What a chickenshit," Judd Grimm muttered. "Why don't he jist lick their asses?"

With one smooth motion, Jessie unholstered her Colt, aimed it at Judd Grimm's crotch, and cocked the hammer. Fear widened the outlaw's eyes.

"You . . . you wouldn't," Judd Grimm sputtered.

"One more word out of you, and watch me," Jessie told him in a voice full of steel, with eyes that were cold as ice.

"We'll help you bury your dead," the Captain told the federales. "Then we'll be on our way. Remember, American soldiers did not kill innocent Mexicans. General Alfredo gave us permission to hunt down outlaws from my country who had come to San Pedro to hide."

"We suspected this," Miguel Ramirez said. "The General was known as a corrupt man. His time was running out anyway. We had been

130

making plans to clean out San Pedro ourselves. Perhaps you did us a favor. Perhaps, even, you saved some lives."

"I'd like to think so," the Captain said. "Truce?"

The federale paused, then nodded. "*Sí*. What is done is done. There has been too much killing already. I believe what you tell me."

"Do you want to bury your dead here, or take them back to your post?" the Captain asked.

"We will bury our dead here. That is our way. Where we fight and die, that is where we bury the soldier of Mexico."

"We got any spades?" the Captain called out, and a soldier answered that they had six short-handled shovels. "All right, Jessie, put those two tough guys to some use."

Judd Grimm scowled and started to protest, then he looked at Jessie's revolver aimed right at his *cajones*.

"You heard the man," Jessie said, and showed the outlaws a wry grin. "Get busy."

Under a full moon, they slowly rode across the desert plain. Jessie and Ki flanked the Grimm brothers, with Captain Frederick leading the march, riding just in front of Jessie.

Jessie sensed a brooding anger among the Captain's troops. She understood their feelings. After taking a head count, the Captain had found he was down to twenty-seven men. And they had been forced to bury more of their own back in the gorge. With, of course, a lot of help from the Grimm brothers. The grueling chore of digging graves seemed to have taken some of the mean spirit out of the outlaw brothers, but Jessie knew that wouldn't last long. They were desperate and frightened, because they knew they were going to die eventually. Worse, she knew members of the Grimm gang were still somewhere out there. Maybe even hunting them at the moment, anxious to free the Grimm brothers.

"Let's make camp for the night," the Captain said, and ordered the march to a halt. "We'll stay out in the open. Those hills to the west are far enough away that we should be able to see anything that might try and move in on us. Build one fire, then secure the perimeter."

Jessie wasn't so sure about breaking for camp there. She looked at the broken terrain. The landscape rolled in areas toward the hills, was cut by gullies, she suspected. And there were enough boulders and cactus dotting the desert floor in all directions to hide any enemy who wanted to creep up on the camp.

When she had dismounted and tethered her horse to some brush, the Captain approached her.

"Jessie, we'll escort you and Ki to Goodwill. No argument, please. I insist. I have a feeling there could still be more trouble along the way. Ki told me several of the Grimm gang escaped back at the palace."

"And let's not forget Red Ghost, Captain," Ki said, standing beside Jessie.

"And let's not forget the rest of my boys, folks," Judd Grimm chuckled. "My boys'll make more trouble for you than a bunch of damn Injuns."

"What makes you so sure they even give a

damn about you?" the Captain said. "They're gone, you're here. They're not crazy enough to take on thirty guns."

Judd Grimm sat down on the ground. "Oh, I wouldn't be so sure about that, Cap'n. You see, only me and my brother here know where the gold's hid. You don't think we were dumb enough to cross the border with all them ingots, do ya, risk runnin' into some *bandidos?* So ya see, we hid it near a ranch, near the Santiago Mountains. Saw me a real nice-lookin' dark-haired gal at this ranch, too. Didn't have the time to drop in and introduce myself properly back then. Never know what could happen between here and there. Suspect my boys may have to pay those people a visit. Might wanna keep that in mind, Cap'n, when we head back that way. Know what I'm sayin' here?"

Jessie saw the fury boil up in Ki's eyes. It was clear to her and to Ki that Judd Grimm was talking about the Stinson ranch. Ki descended on Judd Grimm.

"Ki!"

It was too late. Without warning, Ki had wrapped his hand around Judd Grimm's throat. As the outlaw gagged, Ki told him, "If any harm comes to those people, I will personally rip your liver out with my hands and feed it to you." Ki released the outlaw.

Judd Grimm's retching and his feeble-sounding curses seemed to echo out across the desert.

Silently, Jessie watched Ki walk off by himself. She decided to leave him alone for a while. If something did, in fact, happen to the Stinsons, she knew Ki would live up to his threat. Judd Grimm could be right, she thought. She might not get the outlaw brothers back to Goodwill alive, after all.

★

Chapter 13

With fresh and fearsome memories of Red Ghost still lingering in his mind, Ki was not about to let himself fall asleep that night. So he sat up on his blanket, staring off into the darkness of the desert, searching for any signs of life, any movement beyond the camp, worrying about the present and fearing tomorrow.

The camp fire crackled, several yards away from him, while soldiers ringed the perimeter, standing guard, but he wasn't about to trust them to keep an invader as cunning and dangerous as Red Ghost from silently slipping into camp to collect a few more scalps.

Ki looked at Jessie. She was curled up under a blanket. She appeared to be sleeping, but every few minutes she would toss and turn on the hard ground. Then Ki looked long and hard at the Grimm brothers. Both of them were snoring, but Ki wasn't about to trust them, even in sleep— if they were sleeping. He kept his rifle close at hand. Like Jessie, he wanted to see them face hanging justice in Goodwill. But he couldn't stop thinking about Pamela Stinson and her family, afraid that something bad could happen to them as long as any of the Grimm gang was alive and free. If Judd Grimm had hidden the gold near the ranch, as he said he had, Ki was sure that was where the rest of the gang would head. In the morning, he would talk to Captain Frederick about stopping at the Stinson ranch. After all, it was on the way back to Goodwill, so the Captain shouldn't object. If he had to, Ki would ride alone with Jessie to the ranch.

Ki peered at the black lumps of hills far to the west. For the past hour, he had been watching the desert floor in that direction. He would've sworn he had seen something moving out there, only minutes ago. Suddenly, he spotted a shadow in the distance. The figure sat tall on a horse. Ki couldn't be sure, but under the sheen of a full moon, it looked like a white horse. A white stallion!

"Half-White Eyes!"

Ki jumped to his feet, rifle in hand. A second later, Jessie was standing and the whole camp was alert, weapons in hand.

"It's Red Ghost!" Ki heard a soldier call out, his voice edged with fear.

"Hold your fire! Don't anybody shoot!" Captain Frederick ordered.

"He wants me, Captain," Ki said, walking to the edge of camp.

"You? Why?"

Quickly, Ki told the Captain about their encounter with Red Ghost, back across the border.

The shadow sat, motionless, out there on the desert floor, maybe a quarter mile away. Then the voice of Red Ghost boomed and rolled over the camp. It was a voice like thunder, full of anger and vengeance.

"I have seen you! I know you are there! Tomorrow, Half-White Eyes! Tomorrow, Captain Slaughter! You will die! All of you! Apache blood you shed, it will be avenged!"

Out of panic, a soldier began firing his Winchester repeater, but Red Ghost had wheeled and was riding hard for the hills.

"Stop firing! He's gone!" the Captain bellowed. "Don't waste bullets shooting at shadows!"

Judd Grimm echoed what Ki was thinking.

"Shit," the outlaw said. "Tomorrow, he said. You soldier boys are in for a helluva fight, if that's indeed Red Ghost."

"Sounds to me, Ki" the Captain said, "like he wants more than just your scalp."

Under a blazing mid-morning sun, they crossed the Rio Grande. But setting foot on American soil was not about to guarantee their safety. In fact, Jessie knew they faced their greatest danger, their toughest test yet.

She looked behind her, across the muddy waters of the Rio Grande. Maybe a mile south, she saw them.

Apaches.

They rode slowly across the barren plain, spread out in a long line, with Red Ghost in the middle and just ahead of his warriors, sitting tall astride his white stallion, his lance held high in the air.

Since they had left camp at just after dawn, Cochillo Apono and his warriors had followed them, but the Apaches had kept about a mile's distance between themselves and the soldiers.

They marched up a shallow rise. At the top of the rise, Captain Frederick ordered a halt and turned to look at their pursuers.

"Have to say we're in a world a shit, Cap'n," Judd Grimm commented. "Looks to me like there's maybe more than fifty Injuns doggin' us, itchin' like all hell to attack and hang a few White Eyes scalps from their belts."

"Why don't they attack?" Jessie heard a soldier from her left flank ask.

"That's a good question," the Captain said. "Maybe they're waiting for something."

"Like what?" Eli Grimm piped up, his voice quivering with fear.

"I don't know like what," the Captain growled. "More Apaches, or maybe they're waiting on us to crack and run, or maybe turn toward them and fight."

"That many Apaches, meeting them head-on would be suicide," Judd Grimm said.

"Jessie, Ki, do you remember seeing any rifles among them?"

Jessie shook her head, but Ki answered, "I believe maybe ten or twelve of them had repeater rifles."

"Them odds look worse all the time, Cap'n," Judd Grimm said.

The Captain glared at Judd Grimm, but he had more worries right then than demanding the outlaw shut his mouth.

"C'mon, Cap'n," Judd implored. "They attack, don't leave me and my brother tied up like this. Give us a rifle. The prospect of losing my scalp don't really sit well with me."

"I don't give a damn what the odds are, two to one, three to one in their favor, the last thing I'm going to do is give you and your brother a weapon. And your scalps are the least of my worries."

Jessie looked at Captain Frederick. "That town where you found us in jail . . ."

"You mean the town with no name?"

"Yes. It's about a two-hour ride, to the northwest, I think. There's sure to be some extra gunhands there you can pick up."

"She's right, Captain," Ki said. "Even if it's ten extra men, it's ten more than you've got right now. I don't think they're going to wait much longer before they attack."

The Captain nodded, then ordered the march to continue onward for the town with no name.

With the Apaches keeping their distance behind them, Jessie and Ki followed behind the Captain as they rode into the town with no name, to make perhaps their last stand against seemingly overwhelming odds.

Sheriff Rupert Barnes and Deputy Markin were the first ones out in the street to greet the cavalry. They didn't look happy to Jessie.

"What the hell now?" the sheriff growled. "I

ain't got nobody in jail right now for you to set
free, Captain."

"What the hell now, sheriff," the Captain said,
dismounting, "is that we're about ready to be
attacked by fifty or more very angry Apaches."

The sheriff's jaw hung open.

Jessie saw that some of the rubble from the
destroyed cantina had been removed, displaying
ruined adobe walls that looked like the jagged
teeth of some carnivore. Just north of town, she
spotted wooden crosses planted into the freshly
dug graves of the men who had died during the
Grimm gang's attack. She wondered how many
more graves were about to be dug there, how
many of them were going to die in a town without
a name.

"I need every man you've got, Sheriff." the Captain said. "Spread the word. Do it! There's no
time to waste squabbling."

"Damn, what makes you think anybody here's
gonna take a stand and fight for the Army?"

The Captain scowled. "Sheriff, if you want to
get on your horse and run, that's fine with me.
But I don't think you'd get very far."

"Shit, Cap'n, all you had to do was steer clear
of my town. I gotta enough problems of my own,
I sure as hell don't need yours, too."

Jessie and Ki dropped off their mounts and tethered them to the railing. Jessie saw maybe fifteen
horses hitched in front of the five buildings
left standing in the town. Okay, fifteen more
guns, she thought. That would shave the odds
some.

Then she discovered there weren't going to be

another fifteen guns, after all. She counted six gunmen who came outside and mounted up without a word to anyone. They rode at a hard gallop north, out of town, disappearing in the distance within a few short minutes.

Ki just shook his head in dismay. He looked at the Captain and asked, "How much dynamite do we have left?"

Having taken up a position inside the rubble of the cantina, Jessie was flanked by Ki and Captain Frederick. The Grimm brothers sat among the ruins to Jessie's left. The Captain had about a dozen soldiers with him, all with Winchesters. Those soldiers were now spread out among the rubble, with the rest of his troops having taken up defensive positions in the remaining buildings. Sheriff Barnes and Deputy Markin, Winchesters in hand, were crouched beside the open maw beyond the splintered shards of what had been the bar. The nine gunmen who had chosen to stay and fight the Apaches were hunkered in the rear of the ruins.

Thanks to the Grimm brothers, the entire roof had been blown off the cantina. Now the fierce sunshine of midday burned over Jessie, and sweat coursed down her face.

They waited and sweated and listened to the buzz of countless flies swarming around them. The tension grew thicker with each passing minute.

"Look!" Deputy Markin cried out.

Jessie followed the deputy's stare. The Apaches slowly moved across a ridge to the east of town.

She saw lances, war clubs, tomahawks. And she counted about twelve Apaches who toted repeater rifles.

"Hell they waitin' for!" Eli Grimm said. "Why don't they jist attack and get it over with?"

Adrenaline racing through her, Jessie watched the Apaches. Red Ghost made a sweeping motion with his lance, and with a confidence that appeared to border on arrogance, half of the war party slowly rode north.

"They're gonna circle us!" the sheriff pointed out. "This is it, folks! I just hope I live to curse the day you soldier boys came to my town!"

Jessie sensed the tension and the fear among the men edging toward terror. She was afraid also. She looked at Ki, maybe for the last time, she thought. He had three sticks of dynamite inside his sash, and he puffed on a cigar, ready to light the sticks. Ki looked at her, and the ghost of a smile flickered over Jessie's lips. She held her hand out, and Ki took it. She squeezed his hand. Neither of them, she knew, had to say a word to the other. If it was all to end here, then so be it. Both of them had led full and adventurous lives, had seen and done things that few people ever do. The odds were great that they would die here, but they would die together, fighting to the last bitter breath.

Suddenly, war cries ripped the air and Red Ghost's warriors broke from the ridge.

"Hold your fire until they get closer!" Captain Frederick ordered.

Swinging her Winchester up, Jessie drew a bead on an Apache. Dust billowed above the war party as hooves thundered and war cries kept shrilling in the air.

A dynamite stick flared to life in Ki's hand.

"Fire!"

★
Chapter 14

Ki sent the dynamite stick twirling through the air, as rifle fire erupted all around him.

Crimson holes blossomed on the bare chests of more than a dozen Apaches, as the soldiers, the lawmen, and the gunmen of the town with no name jacked levers on repeater rifles and kept firing away like there was no tomorrow. Within moments, the bodies of dead Apaches began piling up beyond the buildings.

Still they charged on.

But they raced into ear-splitting, explosive death.

The dynamite stick bounced into the line of charging Apaches, detonated, and sent Indians and their mounts spinning and hurling off in all directions. Through the roiling smoke, the clouds of cordite, and the churning dust out in the street, Ki couldn't find any sign of a white stallion. He believed that if he could take out Red Ghost, *mano a mano*, maybe the Apaches would retreat.

Maybe, but he didn't think so, judging by what he saw in the next few moments.

Neither the dynamite blast nor the merciless rifle fire pounding them from the buildings slowed the rampaging Apaches down. Through the din of weapons fire, Ki heard war cries piercing the air from all directions around the ruins. They were circling, attempting to seal a ring of death around the town. If that happened, Ki knew that any second the Apaches would break through the defensive perimeter for up-close hand-to-hand fighting.

Rifle in hand, Ki fired away, kicking two Apaches off their mounts with bullets gouging open holes in the chests of the warriors. Beside Ki, the Winchester smoked and flamed in Jessie's hands, as she swept her fire up and down the line of Apaches hell-bent on breaking into the buildings from the front.

Horses, whinnying in panic, snapped their reins free from the railing and began racing away from the battle. Ki only hoped they lived long enough to be aggravated with rounding up their horses.

Ki lit another stick of dynamite with his cigar and chucked it into the Apache charge. From behind, he heard a terrible scream. As the stick erupted and scythed through several more Apaches, Ki whirled, rifle in hand. He was braced for the worst possible scenario. What he had feared would happen had become reality.

From the rear of the ruins, the Apaches had succeeded in their suicide charge. Tomahawks and war clubs cracked open the skulls of a few gunmen, spraying blood and muck and brain mat-

145

ter through the air. As the surviving gunmen fired with rage and tenacity into the group of warriors bounding over the rubble, Apaches fought on with savage determination, even as their brothers were shredded by scissoring lines of bullets. The unceasing crack of weapons fire, the war cries, and the shrieking of men dying in horrible agony was deafening.

Ki, Captain Frederick, the sheriff, and his deputy directed barking streams of weapons fire at the Apaches in the rear.

An Apache let fly an arrow. There was a shrill scream from across the room, and Ki saw the sheriff tumble, the arrow speared through his eye. On foot, Apaches began leaping over the rubble, breaking the defensive perimeter in greater numbers.

The side of Deputy Markin's head exploded from Apache rifle fire. Then a lance was driven through his ribs as he pitched to the ground. Ki and Jessie dropped three Apaches as the warriors ran past the fallen deputy. Ki's senses were choked by cordite and dust, his face smeared with the blood of soldiers who had tumbled beside him in death from Apache rifle fire.

A blurry shadow with a tomahawk appeared in the corner of Ki's eye. He spun as the Apache craned the tomahawk toward the terrified face of Judd Grimm. Cigar clamped between his gritted teeth, Ki shot that Apache in the head. Then, as the Indian dropped over Judd Grimm, brother Eli jumped to his feet. Within three running steps, Ki caught the outlaw and sent him nose-diving into the rubble by clipping him in the legs with one swing of his rifle. He had already decided he would do his best to honor Jessie's wish that the outlaw brothers remain alive until they could swing by the neck in Goodwill.

Ki turned his attention back to the fierce battle with the Apaches. Jessie ducked a split second before an arrow bounced off some rubble beside her. With one shot to his head, Jessie blew that Apache off his horse.

An Apache with a knife descended on Captain Frederick. The Captain grabbed the knife hand, but the Apache fell on top of him, pinning him with his weight. With a look of terror and desperation in his eyes, the Captain unholstered his revolver and emptied three rounds into the Apache's stomach, blood spraying from the Apache's lower back as the bullets ripped through his body.

Ki lit and tossed his last stick of dynamite at a group of four Apaches running toward him on foot. The stick blew, shredding them to bloody meat. The cigar smoke was now making it even harder for him to breathe, so he tossed the stogie away.

An Apache charged Jessie's back. Pivoting, Ki shot that Apache in the face, a split second before his war club would have crushed Jessie's skull. Jessie returned the favor, shooting an Apache looming over Ki's back with a tomahawk.

Suddenly, Ki found there were no more Apaches attempting to break their perimeter. But the warriors didn't retreat. Instead, they began circling the buildings on foot and on horseback, firing rifles and sending arrows whistling through the air. A soldier behind Ki cried out, as an arrow drilled him in the back.

Even as the rifle fire from inside the buildings kept kicking Apaches off their mounts and knocking them off their feet one by one, the warriors showed no sign that they would retreat.

Then, Ki saw him. Just beyond his warriors, to the north edge of town, he spotted Red Ghost. Cochillo Apono sat, motionless on his white stallion, as if no bullets would dare touch him. Ki met the Apache chief's fierce stare. And Red Ghost dropped his lance to the ground, unsheathed his knife, and pointed it toward the cantina ruins. Ki saw that the Apache chief's blade was pointed right at him.

And Ki knew what had to be done. Even if the Apaches retreated now, he knew he'd never have a moment's peace. Red Ghost wanted to fight him to the death, if for no other reason, Ki believed, then to see who the strongest, the bravest, warrior was.

Ki tossed his rifle to the ground and unsheathed his *katana*.

"Ki, what are you doing?" Jessie shouted.

But Ki bounded over the rubble, leaving Jessie and the others to cover his back. Two Apaches rushed Ki from the side, tomahawks raised. With one slashing motion of his blade, Ki gutted open one Apache as the other warrior toppled from his mount, the side of his head erupting in a burst of blood from rifle fire.

"No!" Red Ghost boomed at two warriors who drew beads on Ki with their rifles. "His scalp will belong to Cochillo Apono!"

As Red Ghost sidled his stallion several yards away from the raging battle, Ki ran in all-out sprint for the Apache chief. If a bullet or an arrow struck him down now, then, Ki decided, that was what was meant to be. With grim single-minded, murderous intent, he left his feet and barreled into Red Ghost. Locked in each other's arms, Ki and Red Ghost hammered to the ground. With their hands locked on each other's weapons, they grappled and rolled through the dust. A look of depthless rage filled Red Ghost's eyes, as he bellowed a war cry, then drove a head-butt off the side of Ki's eye. A blinding white light exploded in Ki's sight, and he felt Red Ghost driving a knee into his gut. Before he knew it, Ki found himself being hurled through the air. He was amazed at the strength and speed of Red Ghost, but this was no time to be admiring an enemy who meant to kill him and take his scalp as a trophy.

With catlike grace, Ki leapt to his feet. Somehow his sword had fallen from his hand, and he saw his *katana* lying in the dust several feet away. He had no time to get to his sword as Red Ghost attacked. He stepped back as the Apache chief swiped at his midsection with his blade. Then Ki cracked a hook-kick off the Red Ghost's jaw, staggering him. A reverse spinning kick to his Apache enemy's head, and Ki sent him sprawling to the ground.

Then it became obvious that one of Red Ghost's warriors was not going to heed his chief's warning. The Apache swung his Winchester around and drew a bead on Ki. Ki reached for his holster, but found it empty. He realized then that the

Remington had flown from his holster when he'd rammed Red Ghost from his mount. He had started to reach for a throwing star, his last and only hope of saving himself, when suddenly the Apache with the rifle spun and toppled, blood spurting away from his chest. One glance in the direction of the cantina ruins, and Ki spotted Jessie's smoking Winchester aimed his way.

A ferocious-sounding war cry from behind, and Ki whirled, cracking a side-kick off Red Ghost's jaw and driving the chief to the ground again. But no sooner had Red Ghost fallen, than he was on his feet, circling Ki, crouched, and swiping the blade at Ki's stomach. Ki slashed a right off Red Ghost's jaw, snapping the chief's head sideways. As he lunged for the Apache's knife hand, the blade rushed at his face. Forced to throw himself backward to avoid having his eyes ripped out, Ki stumbled and fell on his back.

The taste of fear in his mouth, Ki looked up, and saw Red Ghost running at him, the knife raised over his head. Ki felt something jabbing into his spine. As Red Ghost left his feet to descend on him, Ki grabbed his sword from under his back. He thrust the blade up as the Apache chief seemed to fall toward him from straight out of the sky.

"Ki!" Jessie yelled, as she saw the Apache chief plunging for Ki, his blade poised over his head to stab Ki in the chest.

Because of the drifting clouds of dust and gunsmoke, Ki and his adversary were only shadows on the ground in her grim sight. All around her, rifles continued firing and pounding the surviving Apaches into bloody death. Jessie saw an Apache hurl a lance in her direction. She ducked, and the lance sailed over her head. Together with Captain Frederick, she shot that Apache off his mount.

Then she turned her fear-filled stare toward the figures of Ki and Red Ghost on the ground. There was something sticking out of the Apache chief's back. Then, through an opening in the wafting sheets of dust and gunsmoke, she saw Ki roll the body of Red Ghost off of him. Ki stood, sword in hand. Jessie heaved a deep sigh of relief.

As Ki retrieved his Remington, then crouched and began firing with his revolver at the Apaches still circling the buildings, Jessie rejoined the battle. She didn't know how many Apaches were left to fight, but their number had been decimated. Once again, she knew, the dynamite had helped turn the tide of battle in their favor when the odds had been stacked against them.

With their chief now dead and the bulk of their warriors gone to the Happy Hunting Ground, Jessie saw the Apaches retreating.

Three Apaches raced their mounts up the rise to the east. They were shot in the back by the soldiers, and toppled to the blood-soaked soil of the town with no name. Several other Apaches escaped, unscathed.

Captain Frederick ordered the shooting to stop.

Jessie stood and walked out of the rubble, her smoking Winchester fanning the carnage around her for any signs of movement.

She found nothing but the dead.

Slowly, one by one, the soldiers walked out into the street.

It was over.

It was well into late afternoon when they were finally ready to leave the carnage behind them in the town with no name. Jessie and Ki had helped the Captain and his surviving men bury more dead soldiers, as other troops rounded up horses that were scattered around and beyond the town. Jessie had forced the Grimm brothers to bury the lawmen. Another soldier had died from his wounds after the battle was over. The Captain was down to fourteen soldiers. The gunmen who had died during the fighting with the Apaches were also buried in shallow graves. Three gunmen had survived, and when they finished helping to bury the dead, they rode out of town without a word to anybody. The Apaches were left where they had died. It was Captain Frederick's opinion that any Apaches out there would come back for their fallen brothers, and they could take care of their own.

"Waste a damn time," Judd Grimm growled, sweat coursing down his face as he tossed the spade at the Captain's feet. "A few of them Injuns ran. They come back for their dead chief, they might just dig up your soldier boys and scalp 'em for the hell of it."

Captain Frederick said nothing.

Ki asked to speak to the Captain in private. Jessie followed Ki and the Captain away from the others. She knew what Ki wanted to talk to the Captain about. She listened as he explained his fears about the Grimm gang riding to the Stinson ranch, how he wanted to at least go to the ranch to make sure the family was safe. The Captain seemed to think long and hard about Ki's concern.

"They're good people, Captain," Jessie said. "They helped us. I believe the ranch is on the way back to Goodwill. What'll it cost us? A few more hours?"

"He told us that's where the gold was buried," Ki urged. "I'm sure they'll ride to that ranch. Don't ask me why I think that, it's just a bad gut feeling. I wouldn't be surprised if the four who escaped back in San Pedro have seen us at some point and know we have the Grimm brothers. Well, Captain?"

The Captain looked up at the buzzards circling over the town with no name. "Okay," he told Ki and Jessie.

When everyone had mounted, Captain Frederick led the march out of town in solemn silence.

As they rode north, Jessie kept grim attention focused on the vast, barren plain, searching for any signs of Apaches. She saw nothing moving in any direction.

"How many of them Injuns got away, Cap'n?" Judd Grimm asked.

"Not enough to come at us and make a fight of it, if that's what you're worried about."

"You hope they don't come back," Eli Grimm growled. " 'Preciate you lettin' us defend our own scalps back there."

"Why don't you two just shut the hell up?" the Captain said in a weary voice. "Or you can walk."

It was almost two hours later, as the sun began to set beyond the hills to the west and shadows were stretching over the plain, when Jessie saw the figure in the distance. He rode to within several hundred feet of the cavalry and reined his mount in.

"Who's that?" a soldier asked.

"Not Apache," another soldier pointed out. "He's a white man."

"Hey! Judd! Eli!"

A mean smile cut Judd Grimm's lips as he peered at the man on the saddled horse. "Bob? That you?"

"Yeah, it's me all right, Judd. Don't anybody shoot! Don't anybody get any closer!" Bob Feller yelled across the plain. "You see, soldiers, there's a little ranch a few miles from here. We ain't killed nobody there yet. But here's what I want. You ride there behind me. Keep your distance. I don't get back, well, I don't have to tell you what'll happen to those people. Now, when you get there, you release Judd and Eli. We let those people go. We know you got Judd and Eli, soldiers. We seen ya fightin' them Mexicans in the gorge. Just real glad you made it this far."

Jessie saw the rage fill Ki's eyes as Judd Grimm chuckled.

The Captain heaved a breath and looked at Ki. "Well, Ki, looks like your gut feeling was right."

Ki looked at Judd Grimm, and in an icy voice,

he told the outlaw, "Remember what I told you last night."

Riding hard, Bob Feller vanished over a rise in the distance as Captain Frederick gave the order to move out.

★

Chapter 15

As they stopped along the edge of the rise and looked down at the Stinson ranch, Jessie could sense the rage in Ki about to erupt in violence.

There didn't appear to be any signs of life below them, but then Jessie spotted a figure walking out in front of the ranch. He was a dark shadow, standing in front of the place, as the sun had almost disappeared by now beneath the hills to the west.

"Who's in charge up there?"

Jessie recognized the voice of Bob Feller as it lashed through the tension around her, emanating from Ki and the soldiers.

"I'm Captain James Frederick. You have hostages, you said. I want to see them first before there's any sort of negotiating."

"There ain't gonna be no talking, Captain!"

"There'd better be! Or you won't get these two back. And if you don't get them back, you don't get any gold! And if you kill those people, we'll come down and clean up! None of you will walk away! I'll leave you for the damn buzzards!"

Bob Feller appeared to think about something for a moment, then wheeled and hollered through the doorway, "Jimmy, bring 'em out."

Moments later, as Jessie wiped sweat off her brow, she saw three outlaws herding the Stinson family out in front of the ranch. She counted the three brothers, the grandfather, and Pamela Stinson. All five Stinsons had rope wound around them, binding them together as a family.

"Okay, you see 'em, so send down Judd and Eli! Take 'em back inside!" Bob Feller told the other three outlaws.

"Stall them, Captain," Ki urged.

"How?"

"I don't know, but if you can keep them talking, Jessie and I can circle behind the ranch and come up on them from behind."

"You're crazy, boy," Judd Grimm said. "They'll shoot those people dead before you can git within five feet of 'em."

"Excuse me," Ki said to no one in particular, then pulled kerchiefs off the necks of two soldiers. Ki dismounted and shoved a kerchief each into the mouths of the outlaw brothers. "It's not you they give a damn about anyway. It's the gold they want. You're damn fools if you think otherwise. Okay, that's your angle, Captain. Talk to them about the gold."

"I don't know how you put me in a position to keep giving in to your demands, Ki. I can't say I really like it, especially not after all the men I've lost. But I've seen you and Jessie in action. You're both more than capable."

"The two of us are going in, Captain," Jessie

said. "It will make it quick work; they'll never see us. You know all of us together can't just charge that ranch. Now that these two have had their mouths quieted, they can't shout any warning to the others. Trust us to do this. Please. Just this one last time, do what Ki asks."

"All right, Ki, I'll do it your way. You've got twenty minutes, then I'm coming down there with my troops."

"Twenty minutes should be enough time, Captain. Thanks," Ki said. "And wish us luck."

After circling the ranch to the west, Jessie and Ki dismounted and tethered their horses to brush in a gully in the hills. In the dark shadows of dusk, the ranch was now just a black lump, less than a hundred yards below them.

Other than several horses milling around in the corral, Jessie didn't see any movement in back of the ranch. In the distance, she saw the line of soldiers atop the ridge to the south. She heard Captain Frederick's voice, booming over the ranch.

"I know what it is you want in there! You want the gold! I'm trying to find out now where he hid the gold!"

"Quit stallin', Captain, just send them down! I'm giving you all of another five minutes! Then I start shooting one of these people every five minutes you don't do what I tell you!"

"But I'm trying to tell you, you can have the gold for yourselves! A four-way cut is better than six. Just leave me with the Grimm brothers! I want to take them to justice. The rest of you can ride."

"Don't bullshit me, Captain. What are you saying? They gonna pay for the crimes all of us committed! I find that hard to swallow! Only they know where the gold is! They snuck off one night when we passed here and hid it in them hills!"

"I already know that!"

"What are you gonna do, Captain, beat it out of 'em!"

"If I have to! They're facing the hangman! I might be able to strike a bargain with them. They might not swing if you'll just give me a few minutes to talk to them!"

"Come on, Jessie," Ki said, unsheathing his sword. "You heard him, five minutes."

Silently, swiftly, Jessie and Ki moved down the hills and closed on the corral. They angled up on the ranch. Pressed against the wall, side by side, they moved up on the back entrance to the ranch. Her revolver in hand, Jessie could still hear the Captain stalling Bob Feller. She could also hear a note of suspicion in the outlaw's voice.

Suddenly, the back door creaked open, and a shadow appeared in the doorway, several feet ahead of Jessie and Ki. The outlaw turned and spotted Jessie and Ki, his mouth open to shout a warning. With a lightning attack, Ki speared his sword through the outlaw's chest and slid the *katana* free. The outlaw's body crumpled in the doorway.

Beside Ki, Jessie dashed down the hallway. Ahead, she saw the faint glow of light from a kerosene lantern and spotted the Stinson family in the middle of the living room.

An outlaw appeared around the corner. "What

the hell! Bob, we're being attacked!"

It was the last thing that outlaw ever said. Ki threw a *shuriken*, and a heartbeat later there was a sickening crack of bone as the throwing star speared into the outlaw's temple. Crouched at the corner of the hallway leading to the living room, Jessie unleashed two bullets from her .38, drilling another outlaw in the chest and kicking him into the fireplace. She started to turn her aim on the shadow that was Bob Feller standing in the front doorway.

She didn't have to fire off another shot.

Suddenly, a barrage of rifle fire cracked from the hills. Bob Feller danced and jerked in the doorway under the hail of lead ripping apart his chest, shattering his skull.

With his sword, Ki cut the Stinson family free.

"Ki! It's you!" Pamela Stinson cried, and threw her arms around Ki.

Moments later, Captain Frederick and his soldiers poured through the doorway, rifles and revolvers fanning the room.

"It's okay," Jessie told them. "It's over. All of them are dead."

"I can't tell you, Jessie, Ki, Captain Frederick, and the rest of your men, how much I thank you for gittin' rid of this vermin," Grandfather Stinson said. "They came outta nowhere, slithered right in here like rattlesnakes, and held us at gunpoint 'fore we could even spit. Said you was headed this way and they were gonna kill us all if they didn't git the Grimm brothers back."

Jessie stood beside Ki as the soldiers dragged the

bodies of the dead outlaws outside. She sensed the fire between Ki and Pamela Stinson, but she could also tell Ki was trying to rein in his libido out of respect for the Stinson men. Ki would make eye contact with the woman, but break away from her stare before their looks for each other made it all too obvious what was on their minds. Grandfather Stinson told Captain Frederick that they could feed and water their mounts out back. Pamela said she'd cook up some food for everyone.

"My home is your home, Captain," Grandfather Stinson said. "Why don't everybody stay and eat. You can make camp maybe outside for the night and head out in the mornin'. I got a few spare rooms. I can put some of your men up. Hell, maybe the livin' room's big enough to get everyone in outta the cold."

Before she left the living room, Pamela Stinson stopped, turned, and gave Ki a hopeful look.

"That's very kind of you, sir," the Captain said. "But we've had a long, hard ride. If you don't mind, we can accept the food and taking care of our mounts, and maybe an hour's rest, then I think we need to get those other two outlaws to Goodwill. The trouble here is over. And I would like to put our own troubles behind us as soon as possible."

Grandfather Stinson nodded and said he understood.

"Ki," Pamela called out. "Can I talk to you for a minute?"

"In a few minutes, yes, but I have something to take care of outside first," Ki told her, as a quick, disappointed frown shadowed Pamela's face. "Come on, Jessie, let's go talk to the Grimm brothers."

Ki took one of the kerosene lanterns. Outside, Jessie followed Ki to the brothers.

"Well, Judd, Eli," Ki said, "looks like your last hope of freedom just bit the dust."

Judd Grimm spat on the ground, muttered a curse.

"Tell you what, though," Ki said, "let's go find that gold. You can at least look at it and dream what might have been."

Suspicion flickered through Judd Grimm's narrowed gaze. "Why should I take you to it? So you and the bitch here can have it?"

Ki's expression hardened. "We don't need the money, Judd. But maybe, if gold is what you love most in life, I might let you keep a few ingots so you can buy yourself a nice last supper in Goodwill."

Judd Grimm scowled, looked set to tell Ki to go to hell, then grunted and nodded. "Awright. Maybe the sheriff there'll let me and Eli buy a whore for the night. Come on."

Jessie and Ki walked the Grimm brothers away from the ranch, toward the hills in the west.

"It's up here," Judd Grimm said, his voice edged with excitement as he led Jessie and Ki up a gully. "I remember this gully, it forks at the top. Plus them pile of sticks I left at the bottom . . . Yeah, this is it."

Jessie and Ki unholstered their revolvers and cocked the hammers as the Grimm brothers stopped and bent over a pile of rocks.

"Easy," Jessie warned.

Both brothers hesitated, their hard eyes and grim expressions looking almost demonic in the sheen of kerosene light washing over them. Then, quickly, the Grimm brothers pulled the rocks off the crate, which they had left buried in a pocket of the gully.

"Don't open that crate," Jessie said, knowing they might have left a weapon inside.

Ki made them step back up the gully, then opened the crate himself. Sure enough, Jessie saw Ki pull a .44 Remington off the pile of gold ingots. She smiled at the Grimm brothers as the life seemed to wilt right out of them.

Ki took two small handfuls of ingots and shoved some into the pockets of both brothers. Then he closed the crate.

"You're a bastard," Judd Grimm growled.

"You're just gonna leave that gold there like that?" Eli Grimm asked in utter disbelief.

"I told you, we don't need the money," Ki said.

Back at the ranch, Jessie, Ki, the soldiers, and the outlaws ate beef stew. Jessie was famished, and the food was delicious. Pamela Stinson was a good cook. The meat was tender and spicy, and the vegetables melted in her mouth. At one point before leaving, Jessie saw Pamela Stinson manage a few minutes alone with Ki. They talked in the living room.

Outside, as everyone mounted and the bodies of the outlaws were hog-tied to spare mounts, and the Stinsons once again thanked them all for their help, Jessie sidled up to Ki.

"Well," Jessie said, grinning. "She's also a good

cook. Did you tell her you might come back for a little more hospitality?"

Ki chuckled, shook his head. "After all we've been through, don't you think I've earned a little fun?"

Jessie nodded. She couldn't have agreed more. She was just glad both of them were alive.

★

Chapter 16

It was well into the night, with dawn only a couple of hours away, when they reached the town of Goodwill. Jessie and Ki flanked the Grimm brothers, both of whom looked more afraid than ever now that the moment of justice had arrived. With his troops bringing up the rear, Captain Frederick led the march down the wide dirt street that cut between two long rows of one- and two-story buildings. Dozens of horses were tethered to the railings in front of the buildings, with several buckboards scattered around town. Soft nickering from the soldiers' mounts alerted the town to their arrival. Kerosene light flickered from some of the windows in the buildings; then anxious voices from inside the buildings cut through the clop of hooves as more lanterns were lit. Jessie watched as several townspeople appeared in doorways, lanterns in hand, their voices full of questioning.

The Captain angled the march toward a plate-glass window that read, SHERIFF'S OFFICE. A big, broad figure with a star pinned to his muscular chest appeared in the doorway of the office, lantern in hand.

"I'm Sheriff Howard. Just what brings the Army to Goodwill?"

"The Grimm brothers, Sheriff. I'm Captain Frederick. I believe what I have to say, you'll find very interesting, not to mention a little sickening."

A murderous scowl hardened the sheriff's face as he glowered at the outlaws, then looked at the bodies lashed over the mounts in the rear. "Well, I got a strong stomach, Captain. Word is that it was the Grimm brothers who killed the Southerlands and some ranch hands from the Jenkins spread. We found the bodies by the creek yesterday, found the Southerland ranch just a pile of smoking ash. If they did it, believe me, it won't go good for them."

"If we can go inside, Sheriff," the Captain said, dismounting and hitching his horse to the railing, "you can have our statements. And, yes, the rumor, I'm afraid, is true."

Judd Grimm spat on the ground. "I'll confess. I don't give a shit. Nobody lives forever."

"Speak for yourself, Judd!" Eli Grimm cried.

"Shut up, Eli. Like I said, I'll confess, but you gotta promise me somethin', Sheriff. I got some gold on me, and me and my brother want a meal and a whore before we talk. Do that, you can have the gold and our confessions."

The sheriff looked at the Grimm brothers in amused disbelief. "Sure. When they're drinking cold beer and whiskey in hell. Let's go inside. Sounds like these two will be getting a trial in the morning. As soon as the sun is up."

Jessie and Ki dismounted and pulled the Grimm brothers off their horses. Captain Frederick disappeared behind the sheriff, into the jail office. Jessie heard angry murmuring about the Grimm gang from the townspeople behind her. Something told her the Grimm brothers were going to get a quick march to the scaffold.

"Ki, after we give our statements to the sheriff, I'm going to take a long hot bath. Why don't you find yourself a room and get some sleep?"

Now it was Ki's turn to give Jessie a knowing look. "What about you? I think you need some sleep yourself."

Jessie cocked a grin at Ki. "I don't think I need to tell you I might have company later. I can always sleep sometime tomorrow."

After spending almost two hours giving the sheriff her sworn statement, not leaving out one detail, from their discovery of the bodies hanging by the creek, right up to the hostage incident at the Stinson ranch, Jessie had taken a room on the second floor of the Goodwill Hotel while Ki paid for a room down the hall. Now, as the first light of dawn broke over the town, Jessie was soaking in a tub full of hot water. It felt good to relax, to be out of danger, to be away from the stench of death. No Apaches. No federales. No dynamite. No more killing.

She washed herself from face to toe with soap. She had started to drift off asleep when she heard a knock on the door.

"Who is it?"

"It's Captain Frederick."

A smile cut Jessie's full, ripe lips. She had been expecting, no, she had been hoping the Captain would show up at her door.

"Did you bring a bottle of brandy, Captain?"

"As a matter of fact, I did."

"Just a second."

She stepped out of the tub and toweled herself dry. Naked, she went to the door and opened it.

"I . . . I . . ."

The Captain's jaw hung open as he stood there staring at Jessie's stark nakedness. The hand in which he held the bottle of brandy trembled slightly.

"Come on in, Captain. Haven't you ever seen a lady naked before?"

It took a moment for the Captain to regain his composure, but he finally moved into the room. Jessie closed the door. She was enjoying the startled expression on the Captain's face. Smiling, she padded across the room with smooth catlike steps. She sat down in a chair by the dresser.

"Are you going to pour me a drink, Captain?" Jessie kept the smile on her lips, as he stood there like a statue, desire burning in his eyes. "All the troops tucked in for the night? You mean we've got some time alone?"

"You really, uh, you really want that brandy now?"

"Maybe after. Why don't you . . . take off your clothes and come here to me?"

Jessie felt sexually powerful in a way she had experienced only a few times in her life. She wasn't a woman to sexually dominate a man, but she had the urge to take matters into her own hands. She wanted the Captain to do exactly what she wanted him to do, not hesitate, not ask any questions, just do it.

The Captain undressed. Jessie saw that he was already hard, his big pole sticking up near his belly.

She ran a tongue over her lips and felt the moisture and the heat building up, slicking her between the legs. "Come here, Captain, and kiss me."

He stood over her. She took him in her hand, squeezing his hardness, making him moan with pleasure.

"Kiss me . . . all over," she told him. "And I mean, all over. Sir."

He kissed her on the mouth, his breath hot as fire as he darted his tongue in and out of her mouth. She was intent on making it last like before—No, she wanted him to want her with a fierce desperation. Gently, she pushed him down on his knees.

"Kiss my neck."

He did.

"Now kiss my breasts. Gentle. Easy. Touch them. Suck them."

He did.

She felt her excitement burning through her. He was a man of power, a man of authority, and there she was, controlling the action. It was exactly what she wanted. She ran her fingers through his hair, as his hands and his mouth and his lips worked her hardened nipples. She held him there against her breasts, teasing his pole with long stroking motions, making him squirm, as he sucked her nipples, caressed her firm melons.

"Come on, Jessie, please, I'm going crazy!"

"Not yet. Kiss my legs. Start with my feet. Then work your way up. Let me decide when you can go into me with that big, beautiful pole. Or shall I call it a saber? You can spear me with your saber, Captain. But only when I say you can."

He kissed her feet. She opened her legs, as he ran his lips, slowly, delicately, up the length of both of them.

"God, you smell so good, so sweet, Jessie. You are the most beautiful woman I have ever seen anywhere. Damn it, lady, do you want me to beg?"

A smile danced over her lips as she looked down at him, locking his hungry gaze with slightly laughing eyes. "Oh, the time will come. But I don't think begging is very becoming for an officer in the United States Army. Keep going. Up higher, kiss me . . . there. Tell me, am I a goddess?"

"Yes . . . yes . . . you're a goddess."

She moaned and grabbed his hair, opening her legs as wide as they would go, burying his face on her hot and slippery lips.

"Use your tongue," she told him. "Kiss it like you would my mouth. Gentle. Easy . . . easy."

He did. And Jessie also found herself going insane with desire, as his lips and his tongue and his mouth worked her with a mix of tenderness and eagerness. She told him also to put a finger in her, and he did. She thought she would faint from the waves of pleasure coursing through every nerve ending in her long, smooth, creamy-skinned body. With him using his mouth on her, it felt so good, she wanted to keep him like that forever. She lifted one leg higher than the other and told him to kiss the inside of her thigh. He told her he couldn't stand it anymore, he was going to explode. She told him he better not explode, and guided his mouth to her leg.

Finally, she told him, "Stand up." When he stood, she took him in her mouth, but only for a few seconds, teasing the length of his fleshy saber with light brushing kisses. Standing, taking him in her hand, she led him toward the bed. There, she got on her hands and knees. He spread her cheeks and slowly entered her from behind.

"Slow, go real slow, Captain. You make it last. You may never have me again."

She let him take her from behind for a full minute, then she pulled away from him, his slickened pole slapping his belly. Smiling, she rolled over on her back, took him in her hand, and guided him deep into her. She locked her legs on the small of his back, and he began riding her, in and out, with a slowly mounting frenzy. Sweat drenched their locked nakedness. Jessie dug her fingers into his shoulders, kissing him on the mouth and neck. She told him to stop, that she wanted to get on top of him. With one swift, smooth motion, he picked her up in his long, heavily muscled arms, held her on top of him, and let her thrash and buck up and down his steel-like hardness until she cried out, as one orgasm after another ripped through her. And just as before, even when she had achieved climax, he wasn't finished. He took her from behind. Then he rolled her over and took her from the top. Then he turned her on her side and went in from behind, holding her leg high in the air. After Jessie had had one final screaming orgasm, he erupted into her, drenching her with long, hot spurts.

For long moments, they lay there, sweating, their labored breathing filling the silence in the room.

"You think we woke up everyone in town?" Jessie laughed.

"I don't care. Damn, you are something, Jessie Starbuck. You are a whole lot of woman. I could almost—"

She put a finger on his lips. "Don't make promises you don't intend to keep, Captain."

"Okay. How about one more time?"

She couldn't believe her eyes. She reached down and took him in her hand, found he was as hard as ever. "Why not?" she said, and kissed him with a burning hunger.

They held the trial in the morning, just two hours after sunup. Justice proved to be quick, and final, for the Grimm brothers. They were tried for murder and sentenced to hang by the neck until dead. A scaffold was erected at the edge of town, and ranchers and ranch hands and their families came from miles in all directions to witness the double hanging. The Captain's soldiers were strung out in a line near the edge of the gathered people.

Jessie stood by Captain Frederick and Ki on the boardwalk as the Grimm brothers were led from the sheriff's office at high noon. The outlaws had their hands tied behind their backs. And they cursed the townspeople; they cursed Jessie and

Ki and Captain Frederick; in fact, they cursed everything under the sun, including a god they claimed they didn't believe in. Goodwill was shit, according to Judd Grimm; the whole world was shit, and he raved about the things he would like to do to every woman in that town if he had the chance. The sheriff and his deputy struggled to get the screaming, cursing, and thrashing brothers onto the mounts beneath the two nooses. A priest was muttering an Our Father behind them, but Judd Grimm spat on him. The priest wiped the spit off his face and silently walked off, after saying, "May God have mercy on your souls."

"I can't watch this," Jessie said. She had seen enough death already in the past few days to last her the rest of her life. "How about we go up to my room, Captain, and have a glass of brandy? I'm really too tired for anything else."

The Captain nodded.

Ki said, "I'm going into the saloon to get something to eat. I'll see you two later. I'm not in the mood to watch this either."

Upstairs in her room, Jessie sat down in a chair. Captain Frederick poured her a glass of brandy. Twice, they heard a whip cracking horseflesh. The cursing of the Grimm brothers abruptly ended.

Jessie sat there, sipping her brandy. She was exhausted. Captain Frederick sat down on the edge of the bed. He drank straight from the bottle. They sat there in silence for a good half hour, each of them alone with private thoughts.

There was a knock on the door, and Ki announced his presence.

"It's all right, Ki. Come on in."

Ki entered the room. "You won't believe what I heard from a couple of drifters who just rode into town."

Jessie sat up straight, her body rigid with tension, as she saw the grim look in Ki's eyes.

"What, Ki?" the Captain prodded.

"Well, there's a town named Barlowe, about a two hours' ride east of here. Seems these drifters couldn't stop talking about these six bounty hunters who have been there since last night, spending money on drinking and whores like there's no tomorrow. And bragging about all these soldiers and Mexicans they killed."

The bottle of brandy almost slipped out of Captain Frederick's hand. He stood and said, "I'll tell Lieutenant Hankins he's in charge in getting the troops back to Fort Mason. This is something I want to see the three of us handle. I think we owe each other that much. Don't you agree?"

"Let's ride," Jessie said, heading for the door.

★

Chapter 17

The thirteen false-front buildings of Barlowe baked under a blazing late-afternoon sun.

Slowly, their expressions hard with grim intent, Jessie, Ki, and Captain Frederick rode down the dirt street. It was a desolate place, with manure, teeming with buzzing flies, spread all over the street, or in fresh steaming piles heaped in front of the boardwalk. A hot wind breathed tumbleweed across the street at the far edge of town.

They angled toward a dozen or so mounts hitched to the rail in front of the saloon. Parked before the saloon's railing was a large buckboard. Beside the wagon, six horses were tethered close together. Jessie saw the bloodstains in the buckboard.

"They're in there, all right," the Captain said. "That's the same buckboard they used to haul their bounty out of San Pedro."

Silently, Jessie, Ki, and the Captain dismounted. Jessie heard talking, laughing, and the clinking of poker chips from inside the saloon.

"Jessie, you want to stay in between the Captain and me?"

"Sure."

Wood groaned as they stepped up onto the boardwalk. Sweat trickled down Jessie's face. Her heart raced. A fly buzzed around her Stetson.

She pushed through the batwings, Ki and the Captain right on her heels.

And right away, sitting in the gloom against the far wall of the saloon, she spotted the six bounty hunters. They were sitting at a large round table that was cluttered with cards, poker chips, whiskey bottles, and piles of cash. She recognized Jake Kingston, Zeke Zebulon, and Falo, the humpbacked. The other three bounty hunters she had seen but didn't know by name. Kingston and Zebulon had a whore each on their laps. All six bounty hunters froze, fear shadowing their faces as they watched Jessie, Ki, and Captain Frederick walk toward them. In the heavy silence, Jessie heard flies buzzing all over the room.

Less than ten feet from their table, Jessie stopped, Ki and the Captain flanking her.

Jake Kingston grinned around his cigar. "Well, well, look at this happy trio, boys. Welcome back to the States, Cap'n, ma'am, whatever the hell your name is, sonny."

Zebulon chuckled, but it was a hollow sound, edged with anxiety.

Jessie stared in cold silence at the head bounty hunter. She felt the rage burning from Ki and Captain Frederick, felt the eyes of the other drifters in the saloon boring into the side of her head.

176

The grin faded from Kingston's mouth. He took a deep puff on his cigar, blew smoke, then removed the stogie from his lips. "Hey, c'mon, Cap'n, you ain't still sore about what happened down in San Peedro, are ya? It was war, it was every man for himself. C'mon, you made us ride with you and your boys, what the hell did you expect? We ain't bluecoats. Cut your losses and git on with your life."

"Only six of you left?" the Captain asked.

"Yeah," Kingston said, "seems I lost a couple of boys on the way outta San Peedro. Look, Cap'n, there's plenty of money here. Let's say I cut you and those two in for . . . let's go with two thousand, no, make it two-and-one, three-way split, seven apiece. What do you say? Forgive and forget?"

"You two," the Captain told the whores, "get off them and get the hell away from that table."

The bounty hunters tensed as the whores hesitated, then stood and walked across the saloon, toward the bar.

"Hey, I don't want no trouble in my place!"

Out of the corner of his mouth, the Captain told the barkeep, "Shut your mouth, mister, this is official Army business."

"So, what are you gonna do, Cap'n, put us under arrest?" Kingston said, then chuckled.

In a steely voice that left no room for doubt, the Captain said, "No. The party's over."

A stretched second, then rage filled Kingston's eyes. "Why, you rotten—"

Kingston threw the table up into the air, reaching for his revolver. Before the other bounty hunters could fill their hands with weapons, Jessie, Ki, and Captain Frederick drew their own revolvers and began blazing lead death over the six of them. A din of cracking weapons fire ripped through the saloon as the revolvers bucked and flamed in the hands of Jessie, Ki, and the Captain. Holes were blasted open in the round table. Chips, cash, cards, bottles, and blood flew through the air around the bounty hunters as bullets kept pounding them, spinning them around and slamming them into one another. Zebulon fired one shot, an impotent slug that tore into the ceiling as his tattered shirtfront turned crimson. Jessie, Ki, and the Captain didn't stop firing until they'd spent every last bullet.

Bodies of bounty hunters crunched to the floor.

Smoke curled from the barrels of the revolvers in the hands of Jessie, Ki, and the Captain. As the din of the killing shots faded, the buzzing of flies filled the silence.

Jessie heard boots pounding on the boardwalk. Turning, she saw a short, stocky sheriff burst through the batwings, a tall, lanky deputy right beside him with a Winchester in hand.

"Jesus God!" the sheriff gasped.

"These men were wanted for murder, Sheriff," the Captain said in a cold voice.

"Says who?"

"The United States Army."

The sheriff locked stares with the Captain for a long moment. Then he grunted, scowling at the corpses across the saloon.

"Well, I didn't much like them anyway, Captain," the sheriff said. "Fact, someone said they overheard them braggin' about how many people they killed south of the border. I'll take your word. Long as you three get on your horses, get out of my town, and don't ever, I mean, don't ever let me see you here in Barlowe again. Don't even pass through here for a shot a whiskey."

In grim silence, Jessie, Ki, and the Captain walked past the lawmen. They got on their horses and rode out of Barlowe without even looking back.

When they were a mile out of town, the Captain reined in his mount. "I suppose I should be getting back to Fort Mason. I suppose this is good-bye."

"Maybe for us, Captain," Ki said, "but you two can ride on."

"Where are you going, Ki?" Jessie asked.

"I'm surprised you didn't ask about that gold, Captain."

"I didn't give it much thought. I suppose it's still back there at the Stinson ranch?"

"Yeah," Ki answered. "In fact," he said, and smiled at Jessie, "I think I'll take a couple of days off. That gold will be my present to the Stinsons for all they've done. Jessie, I'll meet you at the Starbuck ranch, say two, maybe three days?"

Jessie smiled at Ki. "Sure. Enjoy yourself. Give my regards to the Stinsons. Don't hurry back. I'm in good hands with the Captain."

Ki nodded, shook the Captain's hand, and said good-bye to him. Then he smiled at Jessie, touched her gently on the face, and told her he'd be back real soon. Jessie watched Ki ride south, a smile on her lips. She hoped he had a good time. He'd earned it. And so had she, she decided.

"Well, Captain, take a lady to dinner?"

The Captain chuckled and showed Jessie a warm smile. "After I bathe and shave. Whatever you want, Jessie, whatever you want."

She urged her mount ahead. "You aren't breaking some kind of Army regulations by not getting back to the fort right away?"

"The hell with regulations. Fact, I'm thinking about retiring when I get back. Might even buy a ranch, settle down here in Texas."

"Careful, Captain. Remember what I said about promises."

"We'll talk over supper."

The smile stayed on Jessie's lips. Talk over supper, huh? she thought. She hoped supper was good. And short. She was looking forward to dessert.

It was early in the morning the following day when Ki rode up on the Stinson ranch. In the distance, he saw someone sitting on the fence, staring off into the hills. When he was within a hundred yards of the corral, he saw that it was Pamela on the fence. Suddenly, she turned. Even at a distance, Ki saw the smile light up her face, saw her eyes beaming with surprise and joy. He smiled back at her.

"Ki! I can't believe my eyes! Is it you?"

"It's me, Pamela."

It was going to be a good couple of days, Ki decided. Maybe he'd even stay a whole week. It had been a long time since he had felt so happy. After the hell he'd been through, even one stolen hour with Pamela Stinson would be a slice of heaven.

Ki kept smiling as he watched his beautiful, dark-haired, ivory-skinned angel jump off the fence and run to meet him.

Watch for

LONE STAR AND THE STEEL RAIL SELLOUT

132nd novel in the exciting LONE STAR series
from Jove

Coming in August!

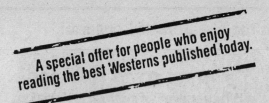

From the Creators of Longarm!

Featuring the beautiful Jessica Starbuck
and her loyal half-American half-
Japanese martial arts sidekick Ki.
